"When the Greens decide to divorce, it doesn't occur to them that their allocation of Mathilda to Mom and Mathew to Dad is the reverse of the twins' own preference—or that each is less willing to give up the other than to give up *either* parent. Unable to persuade their parents . . . the twins bolt to Uncle Ben, whom they assume will take them in. . . . But Ben isn't home; hoping for his return, the twins hang out in Golden Gate Park, where they become acquainted with the various homeless. . . . Meanwhile, the police search for them [and investigate] an ominous series of murders of the homeless in the park. . . . The runaways here are unique, engaging personalities; their experiences enhance their knowledge of themselves and the world. . . . Sachs presents a pervasive current problem with insight and sympathy. A well-structured, thought-provoking novel; a real page-turner."

—*Kirkus Reviews*, starred

# MARILYN SACHS
# At the Sound of the Beep

PUFFIN BOOKS

PUFFIN BOOKS
Published by the Penguin Group
Viking Penguin, a division of Penguin Books USA Inc.,
375 Hudson Street, New York, New York 10014, U.S.A.
Penguin Books Ltd, 27 Wrights Lane, London W8 5TZ, England
Penguin Books Australia Ltd, Ringwood, Victoria, Australia
Penguin Books Canada Ltd, 2801 John Street, Markham, Ontario, Canada L3R 1B4
Penguin Books (N.Z.) Ltd, 182–190 Wairau Road, Auckland 10, New Zealand

Penguin Books Ltd, Registered Offices: Harmondsworth, Middlesex, England

First published in the United States of America by Dutton Children's Books, 1990
Published in Puffin Books, 1991
3 5 7 9 10 8 6 4 2
Copyright © Marilyn Sachs, 1990
All rights reserved

Library of Congress Catalog Card Number: 91-52532
ISBN 0-14-034681-3

Printed in the United States of America
Set in Baskerville

for my good friends
Bette and Frank Pepper

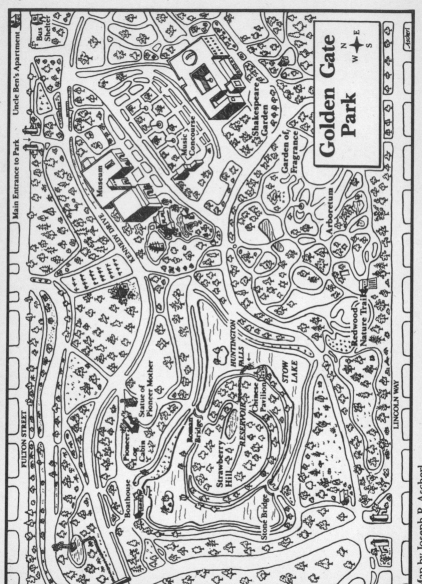

Golden Gate Park

Map by Joseph P. Ascherl

# At the Sound of the Beep

*He lay curled up on the stone bench in the Shakespeare Garden. Even though the early morning fog touched them all with cold, clammy fingers, he was the only one who didn't shiver and snuggle deeper into a sweater or jacket. He was barefoot, too, and wore only a pair of jeans and a short-sleeved shirt.*

*"Look at his hair," said the young policewoman sadly. "It's so pale. It's almost white."*

*The photographer moved around to the other side of the bench and snapped another picture.*

*"I don't like it," said the policeman. "I don't like it at all."*

*"Poor boy," the policewoman said. "I wonder who he was."*

# One

MATHILDA GREEN hated her name. "Why?" she kept asking her parents. "Why did you have to call me that?"

Both of them gave her different answers. Her father generally said, "Because Mathilda was a great queen of England. And you're the great queen in this family." Then he usually picked her up and bounced her around and made her laugh. She liked being bounced around and laughing with her father, but she didn't believe what he said.

Her mother didn't bounce her around and didn't make her laugh much either. But Mathilda did believe what her mother told her.

"We thought we were having two boys," said her mother. "The sonogram seemed to show two boys, so we had boys' names all ready—Mathew—after your father, and either Michael after his father or James after mine. You were a surprise."

"Well, even if I was a surprise," Mathilda said, "you could have given me another name. You could have called me Sandra after you."

Her mother shook her head and twisted up her mouth. "I hate my name," she said. "I never liked being called Sandra."

"It's a lot better than being called Mathilda," Mathilda said. "How would you like it if your name was Mathilda?"

"Actually," her mother said, "I would have much preferred it to Sandra. And then, you have to remember that we hadn't thought at all about girls' names. We had to make up our minds pretty much on the spot. First Matt was born, and we never expected you'd be a girl, so we just weren't ready."

"Well, if I had been a boy, I guess I wouldn't have minded being James or Michael. They're nice, plain names. But I like Bill better or even Ben. You could have called me Ben after Uncle Ben. Weren't the two of you still talking when Mathew and I were born?"

"No, I never considered Ben," Mom said, "and, no, we probably weren't talking then. I think I stopped talking to him when I was about seven."

Uncle Ben was Mom's younger brother. Mathew and Mathilda didn't get to see much of him since he and Mom *usually* weren't on speaking terms.

"Okay, but after I was born, and you knew I was a girl, you could have named me Helen after Grandma Green or Joan after Grandma Burns."

"But Mathew and Mathilda sound so cute together," her mother said.

"I'm going to change it when I get older," Mathilda

said. "As soon as I can, I'm going to change my name."

Unfortunately, she couldn't use her middle name either, since both she and Mathew had been given family names. Mathew was Mathew Burns Green (Burns was Mom's name before she married Dad), and she was Mathilda Foote Green (Foote was Grandma Green's name before she married Grandpa Green).

"Foote is worse than Burns," Mathilda insisted to Mathew. "Kids keep making all kinds of dumb comments about my feet. It's not so bad to be Burns, although I wonder why Mom and Dad couldn't have come up with just a couple of nice, ordinary kids' names like John or Charles for you and Anne or Mary for me."

Mathew said it didn't matter to him. He liked his first name, and he usually didn't use his middle name. Sometimes, though, he might sign his name Mathew B. Green. Mathilda liked to sign her name M.F. Green, and she always tried to get her friends to call her M. But they never did.

Mathilda's best friend, who lived next door, was Jennifer Jane Jordan. She signed herself *J.J.J.* Everybody knew that *J.J.J.* had to be Jennifer because nobody else had three *J*s in his or her name.

"It's kind of boring to have three names beginning with the same initial," Jennifer said languidly one day in April when they were sitting inside her house after school, watching the rain slapping up against the kitchen windows. She didn't really think it was boring at all, Mathilda knew. She was just trying to be kind. "I think it's more interesting to have three different initials."

"I don't," Mathilda said, watching Jennifer take another cookie with her left hand even though she hadn't finished chewing the one in her mouth and still held a piece of it in her right hand. Jennifer ate a lot, and was soft and round all over with a soft, round face and soft, round, lazy features.

"An *M* is nice," Jennifer said kindly.

"It's better than an *F* or a *G*," Mathilda agreed, "but I wish I had three of the same letters like you have. I love to make *B*'s, and *S*'s are okay too, and so are *Y*'s."

Jennifer finished the first cookie, bit into the second and took a third. "Don't you want any more cookies?"

"Uh-uh," Mathilda said. "I'm not hungry."

Jennifer sighed. "That's why you're so skinny. And Mathew too. Neither of you ever seems to be hungry. I wish I wasn't always hungry. Then I wouldn't be so fat."

Now it was Mathilda's turn to be kind. She knew that she was much thinner than Jennifer—taller, thinner and more agile too. She always got picked quickly when they chose up teams at school, and Mr. Halpern, her fifth-grade teacher, said she was a natural at basketball.

Most of the kids said she was athletic because she had a twin brother. But that wasn't true, because Mathew wasn't athletic at all and generally got picked among the last for any team sport. "You look fine," she said kindly.

"What do you want to do today?" Jennifer motioned with her head towards the rainy windows.

"I don't know," Mathilda said. "What do you want to do?"

"I'm supposed to be writing a book report." Jennifer made a face.

"Oh. When is it due?"

"Yesterday." Jennifer giggled. "Do you want to help me?"

"No," Mathilda said. "Let's do something else. You can write your book report after I go home."

"Where's Mathew?" Jennifer asked. "Maybe he'll write it for me. He writes good book reports."

"Mom took him over to the dentist today. His head-gear was hurting him."

Jennifer said, "It's funny how he has to wear bands on his teeth, and you don't."

"What's so funny about that?"

"Well, you're twins but you're not that much alike. I mean you're both the same height, and you're both thin, but he's blond and blue-eyed and he's got crooked teeth, and you're dark and you've got straight teeth. And then you're just different in lots of ways."

"I keep telling you, Jennifer, that we're not identical twins. A boy and a girl can't be identical. I don't know why most people have trouble understanding that. Mathew and I are just like any other ordinary brother or sister. You and your brother don't look alike."

"Mathew is so creative," Jennifer said softly. "Rose Ann Swenson, in my class—you know, the girl with the red hair—I think she has a crush on Mathew."

"On Mathew!" Mathilda couldn't believe any girl could have a crush on Mathew. But she'd noticed that a couple of girls had started calling him on the phone, and that even Jennifer seemed to like talking about him. But Mathilda didn't have to talk about him. It was boring talking about Mathew.

"Let's do something," she said.

"I know." Jennifer grabbed a fourth cookie, and

stood up. "My mother is giving a bunch of old clothes to Goodwill. Let's dress up."

"Okay. What's she getting rid of this time?"

"All of last year's clothes," Jennifer said. "Remember that gorgeous, lacy, pink dress she bought for the opera? She's getting rid of that. And her long cream-colored skirt—that one she kept for two years—she's getting rid of that."

Mathilda loved trying on Jennifer's mother's clothes. Even though they were always too long, she could still fit into them without looking silly. Jennifer, who was much fatter than her mother, had to leave all the zippers open, and in some cases, couldn't even fit into the clothes at all.

"Daddy says he's going to get a divorce if she keeps on spending money on clothes the way she does, but she says for the kind of work she does she has to make a good appearance."

Jennifer's mother owned an employment agency for models in the city, and had been a model herself when she was younger.

Mathilda pulled a soft yellow cowl-neck sweater over the long cream-colored skirt, and slipped her feet into a pair of low, cream-colored boots. She twisted a large bright floral scarf around her shoulders and stood in front of the mirror in Jennifer's room. She looked interesting. She looked better than interesting. The soft yellow sweater brightened up the darkness of her skin and eyes. "Yvonne," she murmured to herself. "Maybe I'll change my name to Yvonne."

Jennifer, twisting and turning inside the frothy pink evening dress, which wrinkled across her hips and drooped around her shoulders, came and stood next to her.

"Oh, no!" she cried, shrinking away from her image.

"Here, stand up straight!" Mathilda ordered, patting and pushing at the pink dress until it floated around her friend's body and set off the pretty, rosy face above it.

"My mother wants me to be a model too," Jennifer moaned, "but I know I never can. I'm too hungry all the time."

"Maybe you won't be when you grow up."

"Oh, I will, I will," Jennifer said. "And besides, I don't want to be a model anyway. I don't know what I want to be, but it's not a model. What about you?"

They both looked at Mathilda's face in the mirror. It wasn't an especially pretty face. The nose was too long and the mouth too wide.

"You've got a great figure," Jennifer said, moving her eyes downwards. "Maybe you could be a model."

"My nose is too big," Mathilda said reasonably.

"You could have it fixed."

"I guess I could."

"And maybe you'd have to let your hair grow."

Mathilda's hair was short and very straight. She reached up and smoothed it. "I'm going to let it grow after the summer," she said. "We'll be in seventh grade then, and I'm going to let it grow long. Maybe I'll be a dancer when I grow up. You can have a big nose if you're a dancer, but you have to have long hair."

"A dancer? How come a dancer?" Jennifer demanded. "You never even took dancing lessons."

"Well, I can, can't I? Anyway, let's change. I want to

try on that pink dress, and you can try on what I'm wearing."

"No," Jennifer said. "Let's do something else. Let's go over to your house and see if Mathew's home yet. Maybe he'll help me with my book report."

# Two

MATHEW WROTE a book report for Jennifer while she and Mathilda played Hearts on the rug in the living room. He went into his room and closed the door so he could concentrate, but every once in a while he could hear Jennifer screaming that Mathilda was cheating. He shook his head. Mathilda wasn't cheating, he knew that. Mathilda didn't have to cheat because she had a true killer instinct and usually managed to win sooner or later at whatever game she played.

Mathew didn't want to write the book report for Jennifer. He wanted to say no, the way he'd wanted to say no the last time she'd asked him. Mathilda had no trouble saying no, and she didn't feel bad either when she did. But he had trouble.

He sat down at his desk and gently moved aside the model of the Discovery shuttle orbiter he had hoped to work on when he came back from the dentist. The headgear didn't hurt anymore, but it made his mouth feel heavy and wet. He got up, opened his closet and smiled at the mirror on the inside door. He could feel a sad lump grow bigger and bigger inside his chest as he examined the smiling face in the mirror. "You'll get used to it," the dentist had assured him. "It's only going to be for a couple of years, and then you'll look like Tom Cruise."

Mathew didn't want to look like Tom Cruise. He just wanted to look and feel like himself. The smiling, metal-banded monster in the mirror didn't look like him. But again he should have said no. When Mom told him it was time to get his teeth banded, he should have said, "No! I like the way I look. Even if my teeth are crooked and stick out, I'm satisfied."

Mathew closed the closet door, returned to the desk, and tried to think about the book report for Jennifer. Last time she'd asked him to "help" her do a report, he'd asked her what book she wanted to report on. "Any book," she said. "Whatever you like." He knew she meant that he should write a book report on a book he'd read. She didn't really mean that he should help her. He didn't say no then just as he hadn't said no now. What he did do was to pick a real easy book, *Ribsy,* by Beverly Cleary, a book he'd read in the second grade. He wrote a sloppy, easy book report, and said dumb things like "Ribsy is a dog. He is a cute dog. His owner's name is Henry Huggins. Henry is a boy. They have a lot of good times together, but sometimes they get into trouble."

Mathew enjoyed doing that report because it seemed to him that Jennifer's teacher would really get angry. After all, Jennifer was in the sixth grade, just as he and

Mathilda were, but each was in a different class, and in the sixth grade, Mathew figured, you're not supposed to do book reports on easy books like *Ribsy,* and you're certainly not supposed to write like a second grader.

"I got an A," a beaming Jennifer told him a few days later. "You're just a sweetheart, Mathew Green."

Mathew licked his bands and looked at the raindrops bursting apart on the window above his desk. This time, he thought grimly, he would do a report that would really nail her, a book report that would outrage her teacher. But what? Mathew got up and moved over to his bookcase. On top of it, a huge model rocket, all set for blast-off, pointed its sleek nose straight up. Mathew reached up and stroked it, feeling a surge of happiness inside him. He had just finished putting the model together a few days ago, and its beauty still overpowered him. He spent a few minutes moving the ground crew back to the farthest reaches of the bookcase, and then worrying that there weren't enough of them just in case something went wrong, he hurried over to his model-train table across the room and tried to find some surplus personnel he could deploy. He selected three of Dad's old lead soldiers and one plastic Neanderthal man—all just lolling around in a Lackawanna freight car—and moved them over to assist the ground crew. The lead soldiers looked silly in their revolutionary war uniforms and so did the Neanderthal man in his loin cloth, but Mathew knew that good help wasn't always easy to come by. That's what Dad always said. He fussed over his arrangements for a few minutes before he remembered the book report.

Just go out and tell her no, he said to himself. Tell

her it's not right. Tell her it's cheating, and tell her you don't want to do it. Mathew moved slowly towards the door, passing to one side of the center island in his room, not really an island but a long thin table holding his model of the Center City Bus Terminal. A couple of years ago it had occupied all of his spare time, but now he hardly noticed it. As he passed, he absentmindedly straightened out one of the blue and white buses in the yard and picked up another lead soldier who had fallen in front of a Coke machine.

At the door he hesitated. What would Jennifer say when he told her no? She wouldn't just accept it pleasantly, would she? Probably she'd argue or say please or maybe she'd even cry. Jennifer always cried a lot. It didn't matter years ago when they were small and all of them cried a lot, but now that they were eleven, it was kind of disgusting. He didn't cry and neither did Mathilda.

Still, it wouldn't make him feel good if Jennifer cried in front of him. Of course if she cried and he didn't see her cry, that was a different story. If he could write a really lousy report and get her teacher to give Jennifer an F, then she might cry—alone in her room—and he wouldn't have to see it. He could know it was happening and enjoy thinking he had made it possible, but he wouldn't have to see it.

Mathew hurried back to the bookshelf and ran his finger along the backs of all the books there. *Model Trains for Boys and Girls,* he read. *Secrets of Space Travel, History of Transportation, Ship Models* . . . "No, no, no," he kept murmuring. He passed over the books he had bought for himself—most of them dealing with models or transportation, the books his parents had bought him—classics he'd never read, and then a group of books that had always stood in his bookcase. Some of them had belonged to his parents when they were kids, but others had just seemed to always be there. Mathilda had a similar number of books in her bookcase— books she'd never read, books that had stood there throughout her life and should have been removed but never were.

*"Latin America Then and Now,"* he mumbled as his finger moved, *"Magic Tricks for Beginners, The Mystery of Light, Chess Made Easy."* Mathew's finger stopped. He pulled out the book and smiled, feeling his headgear straining. Yes, he thought, yes. That's how I'll get her.

Mathew had never read the book and didn't play chess. Cheerfully, he sat down at his desk and wrote. He opened the book only once to get the necessary information off the title page. He even hummed a little monotone tune as he worked. It wasn't any particular song, because Mathew couldn't carry a tune, but he liked to hum when he was happy—working on his models or now—writing a terrible book report for Jennifer.

*Chess is not an easy game to play,* he wrote. *It's not a game I particularley want to play either. I feel the same way aboute this book. It's not an easy book to read, and I don't particularley want to read it.*

*But I was forced to write this book report* (which was true), *so here goes.*

*This book did not help me to play chess. As a matter of fact, I did not read the book at all, and I never will. I would rather read a book on any other subject, even light. There is a book in my bookcase on light and another one on latin america. I'm not interessted in either one, but if I have to do another book report I'll pick one of them, and do it.*

He purposely misspelled three words—*particularly, about* and *interested.* He also did not capitalize *Latin America.* Then he went into the living room and handed the report to Jennifer.

"Here," he said. "I finished it."

They had a fire going in the fireplace, and a big bowl of corn chips on the floor next to them.

"Oh, thanks, Mathew," Jennifer said. She didn't even look at what he'd written. Just laid it face down on the rug next to her, and held up her hand of cards for him to see. "What do you think?" she said.

I think you're going to get into real trouble with your teacher, he thought happily. "Uh, I don't know," he said. "I never play cards."

"Oh, sure you do," Mathilda said showing her even white teeth. She was going to win this game. It was obvious to Mathew, who could see that it was also obvious to Mathilda. The only one it wasn't obvious to was Jennifer. "Sometimes you play, Mathew, and you're not bad at all."

"Come and help me," Jennifer said. "Tell me what I should do with this and this." She pointed to the queen of spades and three hearts she held in her hand.

Tell her no. Tell her you're busy, Mathew said to himself, feeling his headgear holding his head stiff. "I really have to do some . . . something," he said helplessly.

"Oh, come on, Mathew, just for a few minutes," Jennifer coaxed.

"Sure, Mathew, why don't you help Jennifer?" Mathilda said, smiling her killer's smile. "I don't mind."

So Mathew found himself slumping down next to Jennifer, advising her on a number of futile moves and being sucked unwillingly into another defeat at the hands of Mathilda. Not that he minded Mathilda's winning. It was having to be an ally of Jennifer.

A few days later, a beaming Jennifer, waving her book report, hurried into his room as he was putting the finishing touches on his Discovery shuttle orbiter.

"Oh, Mathew, you really are awesome," she cried.

"What . . . what happened?" he asked, hope fading.

"Ms. Berenson gave me an A+. She made me read it to the class. She said it was so funny and original—and independent. She went on and on about that—about how it's important to speak up if you don't like something, and how people will always listen to you if you're funny and original. She said she never thought I was that kind of student but that from now on, if I don't want to write a book report, I won't have to."

"Oh," Mathew said.

"But she does want me to keep writing funny, original things. You're going to have to help me, Mathew."

"Oh!" he said again.

Jennifer couldn't hang around for very long because she and her mother were going shopping. He watched her back as she left his room. No, he said silently to her back, no. I won't help you ever again. No. No. No.

He returned to his model and carefully glued the door in place.

"No!" he said out loud. "No!" he repeated a few more times. The spacecraft needed some people inside, and he thought about where to find them before rising and moving over to the Center City Bus Terminal. He picked up the lead soldier standing in front of the Coke machine and two plastic children with their plastic mother waiting on line for a blue-and-white bus that was going to Washington, D.C.

Mathew fitted them into the spacecraft. None of them could sit, so he had them standing in front of the control panel. The soldier was a little too tall, and Mathew finally moved him to the back of the orbiter and had him looking out of the rear porthole.

Outside, he could hear the familiar sounds of a basketball dribbling on concrete. Mathilda would be practicing by herself in the driveway. He liked hearing the sound of a basketball bouncing on the hard ground and knowing that Mathilda was responsible for it. As long as she didn't ask him to play. He fitted a frame around a window and began humming as Mathilda rose up into the air and tossed a perfect shot through the hoop.

*This year, the rhododendrons bloomed early. The winter had been wet and warm. Reds and fuchsias, pinks and lavenders, whites with delicate magenta hearts—each bush different and unique.*

*But once the petals fell, they mingled on the paths and in some of the hidden places between the high blazing bushes. A child could pick up handfuls of mixed colors and sprinkle them over himself and his mother. She, working seriously with pad and pastels, murmured "Stop it! Why don't you make a drawing too?"*

*The child looked over her shoulder at the vivid colors on her pad and then picked his own up listlessly. He made some quick jabs at the paper with his own thick, colored chalks. It didn't look anything like his mother's drawing, so he soon dropped it and returned to the petals on the ground.*

*His mother, intent on the delicate purple shadows inside a pink blossom, didn't notice. The boy rained petals on himself and then moved off into another private hollow between two scarlet and three pale pink bushes. This time, he rolled on the ground, feathering himself with pink and scarlet petals before moving into another grove of violet, lavender and crimson. That's where he found her.*

*"Mommy," he said, returning. "There's a lady sleeping."*

*His mother frowned and added just a dab of yellow to the pale green leaf she had been working on.*

*"What?" she asked.*

*"A lady," said her son. "A blue lady, fast asleep."*

# Three

ALL THROUGH the month of May, their parents argued. Some months, the twins had observed, their parents argued more than other months. December, for instance, was always a bad month.

"I don't understand why that should be," Mathew said to Mathilda. "Christmas is such a great holiday. Why do they always have to fight about Christmas?

Mathilda was up on a ladder in Mathew's room, pasting stars and planets up on the ceiling.

"Uh, move Mars just a little further to your left," Mathew said. "No, no, that's too far over. Come back a little more. There. That's perfect."

"I never said that," they heard their mother scream. "Never!"

"Yes," their father roared. "You did say it. You always say it. And you always make sure to say it in front of other people."

Mathew went and closed the door. He watched contentedly as Mathilda pressed a sticky Mars up on his ceiling. Now they could work on Venus.

"Maybe it's because they spend a lot of money on us," Mathilda said, turning and sitting on top of the ladder. "Maybe we should tell them they don't have to spend a lot of money on us."

"They have a lot of money," Mathew said reasonably. "Why shouldn't they spend it on us?"

Mathilda nodded and reached out for Venus as their mother shouted, "You're the one who always puts me down in front of people. You're the one who always acts as if you never get anything decent to eat and your clothes are always filthy."

"Well, it's true," yelled their father. "I never do get anything decent to eat unless I make it myself, and the laundry is never done, and . . ."

"Well, I work just as hard as you," screamed their mother, "and I make more money than you do too. Don't forget that."

"There you go again, rubbing my face in it. There!" roared their father.

"A little further away from Mars," Mathew directed. "That's it. That's it."

Mathilda hung around that morning, which was fine. Usually Mathew liked working by himself, but he never minded if Mathilda stayed with him. When they were younger, they played together a lot more, but now she had begun hanging out with her friends and playing basketball or kickball or riding her bike. Mathew didn't have many friends and was happiest working on his models inside his own room.

This Sunday morning, he had decided to dismantle a service station that took up the whole corner of his room next to his closet. You couldn't actually open up the door of the closet because the service station was there. He had put it together four years ago after he'd gotten it as a Christmas present. For a year or two, he had enjoyed buying small models of cars—Porsches, Fords, Mercedes and his favorite, a bright red convertible Ferrari. But in the past couple of years his interests had shifted to planes and spacecraft. He could use the corner to build a space station, and maybe eventually he would take down the bus terminal, too, and use that space as a runway for some of his new planes.

Mathilda finished pasting up the rest of the planets and joined her brother on the floor, next to the service station. She picked up the little Model T Ford. "I bought you this, didn't I? Wasn't it the Christmas before last?"

"No it wasn't. You bought it for me three Christmases ago. That's when I bought you your orange day pack."

"No, no," Mathilda insisted. "You bought me that orange day pack the Christmas before last. And it wasn't orange. It was blue."

"I remember," Mathew said. "It was three Christmases ago. And it wasn't blue."

They argued amiably, which was the way they usually argued. Mathilda helped Mathew take apart the service station, and they were just about to put all of the little cars into a box almost filled with little boats that had been retired from the years when Mathew had been interested in boats, when their mother opened the door.

"Hey," she said brightly, "anybody ready for lunch?"

"Lunch?" Mathew asked. "Is it lunchtime?"

"I can't fit all your cars into this box," Mathilda said. "We're going to need another box."

"Dad and I thought it might be fun to go to Burger King."

"Oh . . . well, okay," Mathilda said without much enthusiasm. But she put down the cars she was holding and stood up.

"Uh . . . well, I just want to finish putting these cars away," Mathew said, "and then I thought I'd move a few things around. . . ." He didn't want to go out for lunch. He didn't like hamburgers anyway. "Maybe you three could go, and I'll make myself a sandwich."

"No," said his father, appearing at the door. "We want you to come too. Don't be such a stick in the mud. You never want to come anywhere with us. All you ever want to do is hang around the house and play with those dumb little models."

"They're not dumb," said his mother. "Everybody else thinks he's a very creative child, but you're always putting him down."

"I do not always put him down. I just want him to come with us. He never wants to go anyplace."

"He's a great kid," his mother shouted, red in the face, fists clenched. "You should be proud to have a kid like him. But no, just because he's not interested in your *dumb* football and he doesn't like going to games . . ."

"I'll come. I'll come," Mathew said. "I can work on all of this later."

Mathew tried hard to make his father happy that day.

He always felt guilty about disappointing his father, so even though he wasn't hungry, and certainly wasn't hungry for a hamburger, he tried to appear enthusiastic when Dad handed him a huge platter with a gigantic hamburger and a side order of fries.

He poured ketchup over it and relish, and tried to assume an expression of boyish glee as he bit into it. A piece of the meat got stuck in his bands, and he moved his tongue carefully around, jabbing at it to get it dislodged. But it jammed in even further. Don't notice it, Mathew said to himself. Just take another bite, and later, when you get home, you'll poke it out with a toothpick.

So he took another bite and congratulated himself on not irritating his father. And it really wasn't so hard, Mathew reflected as he slowly chewed his greasy hamburger, to eat food you didn't particularly like. There were certain helpful rules to follow.

1. Don't look at the food.
2. Don't think about it as you eat it.
3. Pretend you are somebody else.

Mathew looked over at Mathilda. She was poking at her hamburger, separating the meat from the bun and dipping pieces of it into mustard. He didn't care for mustard and decided not to pretend he was Mathilda. He knew he wouldn't pretend he was either Mom or Dad, and he raised his eyes thoughtfully to the ceiling as he tried to make a decision.

Of course. He would pretend to be Uncle Ben. Uncle Ben was a vegetarian and never ate hamburgers, so he was always a good one to pretend to be.

Mom said, ". . . the last two weeks of August. That's

the only time I can get away. Marcie and Linda will be gone in July, and Harry—the selfish pig—is taking all of August." Mom sold real estate and had become the best salesperson in her office.

"August is no good," Dad said. "I can't get away until October."

"October!" Mom put down the uneaten part of her hamburger and glared at him. "What good is October? The kids will be back in school. I'm not going to take them out of school just for a lousy family vacation. You never think about us when you work out your vacation plans."

"Sandra," Dad said in his controlled voice, "you know that we're remodeling the store in Los Angeles. You know it. I've told you twenty—no—thirty times."

Dad owned two sporting-equipment stores. One was in town and the other in Los Angeles.

"You're always remodeling that store," Mom said, waving a limp french fry around. "You pour more money into that store than you'll ever get out of it. Close it! It's a bust! I keep telling you."

"It's not a bust," Dad said, putting down his hamburger and leaning forward. His face was red, and beads of sweat dotted his forehead.

"Uh . . . could somebody pass me a napkin?" Mathew asked.

"It is a bust," Mom insisted. "But it gives you a chance to get away from us. You'll do anything to get away from your family."

Neither of them seemed to notice whether or not Mathew was eating his hamburger, so after a while, he was able to get up, carry the uneaten part of it off to the men's room, toss it out and work away with a toothpick at the piece of meat caught inside his bands.

When he came back to the table, both of his parents were eating the remains of their hamburgers while Mathilda was trying unsuccessfully to get them interested in plans for the school picnic.

Mom and Dad definitely argued more that May than any other month. One night, Dad didn't come home at all, and Mom said he'd gone to Los Angeles. But when he didn't come home for four or five days, Mathilda said, "Something's up."

"What?" Mathew asked.

"I don't know, but did you see her eyes this morning—all red and swollen?"

"She has hay fever," Mathew said. "Her eyes always get red and swollen in the spring."

"Not like this," Mathilda said. "Something's wrong."

"I don't think so," Mathew insisted. "They always fight a lot. I guess most parents do. I don't know why, but they do."

At the end of the month, Dad returned. He tossed Mathilda around and made her laugh, and he came in to Mathew's room, sat down and showed a great deal of interest in the model P47 Thunderbolt that Mathew was working on.

That night, Mom fixed the kind of dinner both twins liked—ravioli, salad and crisp French bread. They had ice cream sundaes which they made up themselves with either chocolate or vanilla ice cream, nuts, marshmallows, chocolate syrup and maraschino cherries. Everybody was so pleasant and interested in everybody else, and Mom and Dad were so polite and thoughtful of each other, Mathew should have been suspicious. But he wasn't. And neither was Mathilda. She was on her way back to the table from making herself a sundae when Mom said, very cheerily, "Okay now, kids. Let's settle down. Dad and I have something to discuss with you."

"Our vacation?" Mathilda asked, smiling. "Can we go to La Jolla?"

Mathilda loved swimming and beaches. Two years ago, they had gone to visit Uncle Robert, Dad's brother, and his family in La Jolla. They had stayed for a whole week. Mathilda spent every day on the beach and had come back with a glorious tan. Mathew, on the other hand, had turned bright red the first day out and had spent the rest of the week sitting on Uncle Robert's shady porch, working on model planes. Both twins had enjoyed that vacation and were eager to go back another time.

"Well, no," Mom said. "Not this year."

"Maybe next," Dad said gently. "We can try next year."

"That's right." Mom nodded pleasantly at Dad, and they both exchanged smiles. "Next year we'll try, if that's what the two of you want."

Mathilda sighed. "Do we have to go to camp again?"

"I thought you loved camp," Mom said. "You came back with a pack of awards, singing all those camp songs. You said you loved it."

"I guess it wasn't so bad. I had Brenda for my counselor, and she was a nerd. Maybe if Connie is there— she was the counselor for the eleven-year-olds—then it would be okay. And I think they teach the eleven-year-olds how to canoe. I guess I won't mind. But Mathew will. He hated it."

"He did?" Mom seemed genuinely surprised. "I didn't know Mathew hated it."

They were all looking at him, and he tried to smile and look cool. But it was a weak, simple-minded smile—he knew that. Yes, he had hated camp, hated all the group activities, and the overnight hikes, and the silly games and songs. If he could have spent all of his time in the arts and crafts shop, maybe it wouldn't have been so bad.

Dad said, a little impatiently, "Mathew, you really have to learn to speak up. If you don't like something, you have to say so."

"It was okay," he said weakly, looking reproachfully at Mathilda.

"Everybody liked Mathew," she said quickly, trying to make it up to him. "He got an award for building the best birdhouse, and the crafts counselor said—"

"Well, well," said his father, smiling at her, "it doesn't matter because this summer, Mathew won't have to go to camp."

Mathew let out a long, comfortable breath. That was good news.

But Mathilda looked at Dad, and said, puzzled, "Mathew won't have to go to camp?"

"That's right," Dad said.

"But what about me?"

"Oh, you can go," Mom said. Then she and Dad looked at each other.

"You'd better tell them," Dad said.

"Tell us what?"

"That we're getting a divorce," Mom said quickly. "We want you to know that, and also that we love you both very much. That will never change."

"That's right," said Dad. "We love the two of you very much, and we always will."

"Absolutely," said Mom.

"It won't make any difference. . . ."

The two of them went on talking together for a while, but then Mathilda broke in and asked nervously, "How come I go to camp but not Mathew?"

"Because," Dad said, "Mathew is coming with me."

Mathew felt trapped and frightened. For years, Dad had talked about how the two of them should take a vacation together. Dad liked to tell about how his father had taken him and Uncle Robert on fishing trips out in the country—how they'd slept out and fished all day and cooked their fish at night over an open fire. How they'd laughed and talked and loved being free and away from the world of ordinary people.

For years Mathew had dreaded the thought of going alone on such a trip with Dad. He didn't think he'd enjoy fishing—watching a struggling fish writhing at the end of a fishing pole with a painful hook in its mouth. He didn't think he'd like that, but even worse was the worry of being alone with his father and not knowing what to talk to him about. It was too bad he couldn't be the kind of son his father wanted.

But he tried to pull himself together. His father, no doubt, wanted to spend a summer vacation with him before the big separation. He didn't want to upset his father and was trying to compose his face into an expression of pleased acceptance, when his father said, "I'm going to be moving down to L.A. as soon as school ends. Mathew will come with me, and Mathilda, you'll stay here with Mom. Of course, you'll both spend lots of weekends together. From time to time, maybe we can switch off and—"

"No!" said Mathew.

"What?" his father asked. "What did you say?"

"I said no!" said Mathew. "No! No! No!"

# The Inquiring Reporter

*How do you feel about the homeless?*
(Asked in Golden Gate Park)

**Greg Osborne, 47, telecommunications manager, San Francisco**

Angry and disgusted. Most of them are alcoholics and druggies who don't want to go to work. There are plenty of jobs around if you're not lazy. They should be put on a plane and shipped off to Alaska. Why does San Francisco always have to end up with the rejects?

**Margaret Chin, 32, secretary, San Francisco**

It's really a crime that people have to end up on the streets. You see families with little children. Our government should stop sending people off into space and solve the problems we have here on earth. Nobody should have to live out on the streets.

**Rose Donovan, 57, housewife, San Francisco**

Scared. I've lived here all my life, and when I was a kid I could come here to the park with a little friend and play safely. My mother never had to worry about me. Now it's not even safe to walk here in broad daylight. You've got all those homeless people living in the bushes. And they're dangerous. Did you read that they found a second body in the park last week?

# Four

IT DIDN'T MATTER what his parents said, Mathew just kept saying "No!"

Mom talked and talked to him that night. Long after Mathilda had gone off to sleep, and Dad (in the guest room) had gone to sleep, Mom stayed with him talking.

"I know this is hard for you, darling," Mom said, trying to pull him closer to her, "but it will only be for a while. Maybe we can change off from time to time, and you can be with me, and Mathilda will go—"

"No!" Mathew said, shaking his head. "No!"

Mom's face softened. She tried to smile at him, but tears welled up in her eyes. He quickly looked away but could hear her fumbling around in her pocket for a tissue. It took a few minutes before she was able to continue.

"Mathew, darling," she said, "you know I love the two of you just the same. But Dad loves you both, too.

So it has to be that one of you goes with him, and one of you stays with me. It seems more sensible that a boy should go with his father, and a girl stay with her mother. You understand, don't you, darling?"

"No," Mathew said, and now the tears began rolling down his face. He put up his arm and wiped his eyes on his sleeve, feeling the wetness spreading to the side of his head. Even in the midst of his upset, he felt amazed that, finally, he could say no. And how easy it was to do so. "No!" he said again. "I won't."

Mom moved closer to him. They were both sitting on his bed, and she had to push aside some bits and pieces of the new model P47 Thunderbolt he had been work-ing on. "I know you're probably worried because . . ." Mom hesitated. He looked up into her wet face, and then quickly looked away again. If he had to choose one parent over the other to stay with, he guessed he would pick her. But there was something more impor-tant he had to explain to her.

". . . worried," she continued, "because . . . well . . . you think Dad isn't going to let you continue—well, continue, you know . . . being the way you like to be."

Mathew wiped the other sleeve across his face, and his mother put an arm across his shoulder and pressed her fingers so hard that his whole arm hurt. "But you don't have to worry. Dad sometimes is a little thought-less, but he really loves you very much and is very, very proud of how handy you are. You'll probably both stay with Grandma and Grandpa Green until Dad finds a place, and he says you can bring as many of your mod-els down there as you like. You'll have Dad's old room—that nice big one over the garden, and you'll come home, I mean, you'll come back here often— maybe even every weekend in the beginning if you like. I know you'll miss me. I'll miss you too. But we'll talk all the time on the phone and . . ."

She pulled his head down on her chest and hugged him hard. Her tears fell on his head and neck. She didn't understand, and he tried to tell her, but she was crying too hard and couldn't listen.

Mathilda fell asleep right away. Her parents always bragged about the way Mathilda slept. Even when she was a tiny baby, they said she was the best sleeper anybody ever saw. When she was a baby, they said, she took long naps during the day and slept all through the night almost as soon as she first came home from the hospital.

"Mathilda falls asleep even before her head hits the pillow," her mother said.

That night was no different. She fell asleep before her head hit the pillow, but in the middle of the night, she woke up. Suddenly. Something terrible was happening. She sat straight up in her bed and waited for it. There was a sound she'd never heard before—a horrible sound. It was her own terrified breathing. Nothing else.

She dropped out of bed, hurried into the bathroom she and Mathew shared and tried to calm down. No, no, she thought, this can't happen. It can't. After a while, she washed her face, brushed her teeth and looked at her face in the mirror. Her hair was messy from sleeping, and she grabbed her comb and worked away at it until it lay quiet and shiny on her head. Now she looked like herself. But her mouth was trembling. Was that her mouth? She'd never seen her mouth tremble, and for a second or two she was so occupied by looking at the wonder of it, she forgot the reason. Then she remembered.

She pushed open the door to Mathew's room and rushed inside. At the side of his bed, she stood still, looking down at him. He lay on his stomach with his face buried in the pillow. She couldn't see his face, but all the terrible fear inside of her began to fade. She took a few deep, calm breaths before sitting down on his bed.

Very soon he woke up. "Mathilda?" he said.

"I couldn't sleep," she told him. "I got scared."

Mathew sat up in his bed and nodded. "I tried to tell her, but she didn't understand. She thought I was upset because I didn't want to go with Dad."

"We'll both tell her tomorrow," Mathilda said. "We'll tell the two of them. They'll have to listen to us."

"They won't like it," he said nervously, trying to prevent that old weak feeling of his from taking over, "but that's the way it will have to be."

"Oh, yes," she said, and then she smiled at him. He couldn't exactly see the smile because it was night, and there were shadows on her face. But he knew it was there. "You said no, Mathew." Mathilda began giggling. "You said no, and you kept on saying it."

He started laughing too. Soon they both felt better, and Mathilda went back to her room. Each of them slept very well until the morning.

At breakfast, Mathilda spoke first. She waited until the four of them were seated, and then she said, "Mathew and I have decided that we won't be separated."

Mom poured Dad another cup of coffee and looked at him sadly.

"No," Mathew echoed. "We won't be separated."

Mom passed Dad the cream and sugar, and shook her head. "I was afraid this would happen," she said.

The three of them looked at Dad.

"Why are you all looking at me?" he asked, pushing away his coffee cup.

Their mother said, "Because the kids want to stay together. I had a feeling this was going to happen. I'm sorry, Matt."

"If you had a feeling this was going to happen, Sandra, why didn't you say so before? If I remember correctly, it was your idea for each of us to take one of them. And why are you saying 'I'm sorry, Matt,' as if you're sorry for me?"

Mathew could see that his father was getting angry so he said quickly, "Maybe we could all stay together, even if there is a divorce."

Now everybody was looking at him, and as he continued speaking, he knew his idea was not a very good one. "I mean, it's a big house. Maybe Dad could have the guest room like last night. . . ." Dad snorted and shook his head. "Or maybe we could build a couple of rooms over the garage like Jesse Lucas's family did."

"No," Mom said, "that wouldn't work out at all." She smiled tenderly at Mathew. "You're not old enough to understand, darling, but when people get a divorce they don't want to live in the same house any longer."

"That's right," Dad said. "They certainly don't."

"But, Matt, you'd be free to come and see the kids any weekend you'd like or they could go to you. They could spend vacations with you—maybe even Christmas and Easter."

"Now just a minute," said their father. "How about *you* being free to see them weekends and letting them spend their vacations with *you.* I can take both of them. My parents' house is even bigger than this one, and they'd have the pool. . . ."

Mom spoke slowly, as if she were addressing somebody who didn't speak English. "This is their home," she said. "They've grown up here. They go to school here. This is where all their friends live. And I am their mother. Remember?"

"I remember perfectly well, thank you. And maybe you should remember that I'm their father, and I care just as much as you do about them."

"Well, why don't we just ask them who they'd rather stay with," shouted their mother, very red in the face.

Both of them snapped their heads around and looked at the twins. Mathew knew who he'd rather stay with, but he wasn't sure about Mathilda. The important thing, however, was that they stay together.

"I want to be with Mathilda," he said finally, keeping his eyes down.

Mathilda said, "Yes. I want to stay with Mathew."

"Maybe we could take turns." Mathew tried again. "I mean we could stay here with Mom for a year, and then go with Dad for a year, and then . . ."

"No, no," said their mother. "That would be much too unsettling for the two of you. You'd have to be switching schools all the time, and making new friends. No, no. The best thing would be for you both to stay right here."

"Who says that's the best?" their father demanded. "You're never around. If they were with me down in L.A., my mother—my father too, now that he's retired—would be around to really look after them."

"Selfish! Selfish! Selfish!" screamed their mother. "All you ever think of is yourself."

The twins were late for school that morning. They were late for school the next morning, too, and the next. Their whole daily routine crumbled as their parents battled over custody.

"I'm worried," Mathilda said on their way to school at the end of the week. "We don't seem to be getting anywhere."

"Maybe," Mathew said, "they'll just forget about getting a divorce altogether. Maybe they'll just go right on like they always have, fighting and then making up."

"They never really make up," said Mathilda. "Either they're fighting or they're not fighting."

"If we have to choose," Mathew asked, "who would you pick?"

"Dad," Mathilda said. "How about you?"

"Well, I guess Mom," Mathew said, and then quickly added, "but I'd go with Dad if that was the only way of staying together."

"If that was the only way, then I'd stay with Mom."

"But what if . . ." Mathew stopped.

"What if what?"

"What if they can't agree, and they go back to their first idea of splitting us up."

Mathilda shook her head. "Oh, they won't. Now that they know how we feel, they'll just have to go along with us."

There was only one week more of school when their parents decided.

"I'm very sorry," said their mother grimly, "but your father . . . Well, we simply can't give the two of you up. So we're going back to our original plan. As soon as school ends, next weekend as a matter of fact, Dad and Mathew will go down to L.A. No! No! There's no point in saying anything further now. Your father just won't . . . I mean, maybe after we get a little distance from all of this, we can get together and try to work something else out. But for the time being . . . No, Mathew . . . Mathilda . . . there's nothing else to say. We've decided."

This time, the twins sat on the floor in Mathilda's room, on her pretty hooked rug that Grandma Burns had made for Mom when she was a girl. There was a nearly full moon up in the sky that night, only a little piece missing from one side. The moonlight streamed through the window, outlining them both in a sharp blue light.

"We'll have to run away," Mathew said.

Mathilda looked around her room. Even in the blue light of the moon, everything looked familiar and precious—her bed, her chair, the painting she had done in second grade hanging up on the wall, her books, her old pink sweatshirt thrown on her chest. . . . She didn't want to leave them. A sob broke from her throat. Mathew leaned forward anxiously.

"Yes," Mathilda said. "We'll run away."

# Five

IT TOOK THREE DAYS before they decided, and until they did, Mathilda couldn't fall asleep. For the first time in her life, her head reached her pillow wide awake. She lay on her back with her eyes on the ceiling and considered all the possibilities. From time to time, she would drop off into a fitful sleep where even inside her dreams, she continued considering the possibilities:

1. Grandma and Grandpa Green down in L.A. No good because Mom would find out and would never agree.
2. Grandma and Grandpa Burns in Topeka. No good because Dad would find out and would never agree.
3. Uncle Robert and Aunt Donna in La Jolla. No good because both Mom and Dad would find out and neither would agree. She also didn't think Uncle Robert and Aunt Donna would allow them to stay.

4. Just get on a bus and keep going. No good because sooner or later they would run out of money and be caught.

On Tuesday night, so late it was really Wednesday morning, Mathilda hurried into Mathew's room and woke him up. He had been sleeping very well since they'd agreed to run away, because he knew that Mathilda was working out the details. He felt confident in her abilities.

"We'll go to Uncle Ben's," she said, sitting down on the edge of his bed.

Mathew sat up and rubbed his eyes, waiting for her to continue.

"It's a foolproof plan," she explained. "He and Mom aren't on speaking terms, so he won't give us away."

"But how do you know he'll let us stay with him?"

Mathilda had already thought of that. "Because he doesn't approve of the way Mom is bringing us up. Don't you remember? Last time we visited him, he and Mom got into that big fight over bringing up kids. And he said she was feeding us all the wrong stuff and buying us too many things. He said we were overprotected and didn't know anything about the real world and that if we were his kids, he would do everything just the opposite from her. Well, this is his chance."

"He's right about the food part," Mathew said, "but I don't know about the rest of it."

Mathilda wasn't finished. "And then Mom said he didn't know anything about child raising because he didn't have any kids of his own, and she thought he should just keep his big mouth shut until he did."

"Maybe he got married since we saw him," Mathew said. "Maybe he's even got a kid of his own by now."

"Well, we can baby-sit if he does," Mathilda said, "and we're no trouble. We can help out with the housework, and neither of us eats a lot, and we don't really need a lot of things. He really hates Mom, so I'm sure he'll let us stay. Just to spite her."

Mathew looked around the room at his models and licked his bands. "Sooner or later," he said, "we'd have to let Mom and Dad know we were okay. Maybe we should leave a note and tell them where we are."

"Uh-uh!" Mathilda said. "We can't tell them we're going to Uncle Ben's, because then they'll just come and get us."

"Well, maybe we can just say we're running away and not say where we're going."

"Nope," Mathilda insisted.

"But won't they worry?"

"I guess they will," Mathilda said slowly. "But maybe after a couple of months, once we're all set at Uncle Ben's house, we could tell them where we are. Maybe by then, they'll be used to the idea of us being away. Maybe they'll even like it."

"I don't think so," Mathew said, remembering his mother's tears falling on his head.

"No, I guess not," Mathilda agreed, thinking of her father bouncing her around.

"We'd better leave them a note," Mathew said. "We can just write something like, 'We're running away because we want to stay together. Don't worry about us. Love and XXXs, Mathilda and Mathew.'"

"Where would you put the note?"

"Maybe over the fireplace. Isn't that where people always put notes when they run away?"

"I guess so, but Mrs. Warren comes in to clean the house in the mornings, and she'd see it first."

Mathew hadn't thought of that and said slowly, "Well, we could mail it."

"They'd see the postmark and know where we were."

"Not if we mailed it in town before we left."

"Good! Good!" Mathilda said briskly, standing up. "That's settled then. We'll mail it Friday just before we get on the bus to San Francisco. They'll get the card on Saturday morning, so they'll only have to worry Friday night, and Dad doesn't usually get home until late on Fridays."

After that, Mathilda had no trouble sleeping.

There were a few other details to work out, such as what kind of clothes to take, how much money and whether they should leave before school or after. Friday was the last day of school and also the day of the class picnic.

"Before," Mathilda decided. "We'll act as if we're going to school, but we'll stuff a couple of extra things in our daypacks. I've got twenty-seven dollars, and what have you got?"

"Around forty-two."

"Okay, we'll take the money but nothing else. We'll just wear our ordinary clothes with maybe an extra sweater. We don't want to be noticed."

"Sometimes Jennifer walks to school with us," Mathew said.

"Not lately, because we've been late. She won't wait,

and then if we're not in school, nobody will think anything of it. Lots of kids go off on their vacations the last day of school."

"Should we call Uncle Ben first and tell him we're coming?" Mathew asked.

"No," Mathilda said. "That would be too risky. We'll just turn up at his house, and when he hears what's happening, I know he'll go along with us. He's . . . he's . . ."

"I know what you mean," Mathew said. "He's kind of like a kid himself."

Their parents spoke so gently to each other, and so lovingly to them during the week, that the twins knew their old life had ended. Their mother talked to Mathilda about a special day she was planning just for the two of them. Maybe they'd go shopping for summer clothes, eat lunch in—well, Mathilda could pick the restaurant—any place she liked—and then maybe later they'd go for haircuts.

"I'm going to let my hair grow," Mathilda said.

Her mother laughed and patted her own head. "What a good idea, darling. Maybe I'll do the same." She came and stood next to Mathilda and turned them so that they could both look at themselves in the mirror.

"See how much we look alike," said her mother, smiling.

And they did—Mathilda, dark with her long face and long nose and frowning mouth; her mother, dark with her long face and long nose and smiling mouth. Only the mouths were different. Usually it was Mathilda who smiled and her mother who frowned.

She didn't say anything, so her mother drew her closer and murmured, "We are going to have a lovely time together, Mathilda. You'll see. It will all work out just fine."

Yes, Mathilda wanted to say, it will work out just fine, but not the way you think.

Mathew's father sat with him in his room Thursday night. Which was too bad. Mathew wanted to pack his daypack, count out his money again, maybe write the postcard they would mail just before they got on the bus, arrange all his models in perfect order so that . . . so that . . . He didn't know how to finish the thought. He supposed one day he would be returning to them, and wanted them to know he would expect to find them just the way he had left them.

But first he had to get rid of his father. It was strange to have him sitting there, talking about Sunday when they would leave for L.A.

". . . eleven o'clock flight," his father was saying, "so Saturday we'll pack, but Mathew, I don't want you to feel you have to pack everything on Saturday. Just make believe it's going to be for a long weekend. You'll be coming back lots of times over the summer, and each time you can take a few more things back with you. Mom says she'll help, and maybe you can just tell her what you think you'll want—eventually—but, son, I don't want you worrying about anything."

His father leaned forward and patted him quickly on the shoulder. Man to man. Then he went over to examine the orbiter. His father was embarrassed, Mathew realized, and was trying not to let it show. He felt sorry for his father. He always felt sorry for his father, and he wondered what he could say to make his father feel good. But his father began laughing, so Mathew was able to stop wondering. His father had picked up the lead soldier in Revolutionary War uniform from inside the spacecraft and was shaking his head as he turned, still laughing, holding out the lead soldier in Mathew's direction. "Only my son," his father said, "would put an eighteenth-century soldier into a twentieth-century spaceship."

Mathew smiled weakly at his father, feeling foolish, feeling as he often felt in his father's presence, feeling impatient for his father to leave his room so he could say good-bye to his models.

As the crowded bus pulled away from the depot that morning, the twins turned towards each other and smiled.

"It was so easy," Mathew said. "I never thought it would be so easy."

Mathilda grinned. "Mom even forgot to kiss us good-bye."

"Well, she would have," Mathew said, "but then the phone rang, and she had to go answer it."

"Look!" Mathilda pointed out the window at the sunlight glittering on the ocean waves. "They'll have a great day for the picnic."

"Who cares about the picnic?" Mathew said bravely, knowing he did care.

"That's right," Mathilda agreed, but then she cried out, "Oh, no!"

"What is it?" Mathew could see her stiffen and half

rise from her seat. Maybe she had changed her mind and wanted to get off the bus. What would he do if that's what she wanted? He could feel ripples of panic lacing through his stomach, and he put out his arm in front of her.

"I just remembered," she said. "I forgot my Mickey Mouse watch. It was on my night table, and I was just going to put it on this morning, when I remembered that I had another five dollars in my desk drawer. So I went to get that, and then I forgot my watch."

Mathew settled back in his seat and looked at his own Mickey Mouse watch, a gift from their mother last Christmas. "It's okay," he said, relieved. "Yours didn't go very well anyway. As long as we have one."

"But I loved mine," Mathilda insisted. "I hardly ever took it off. I want my own."

"Maybe Uncle Ben will buy you one."

"He doesn't believe in buying lots of things for kids," Mathilda said unhappily. "And besides, he doesn't have much money anyway."

"I wonder why he doesn't," Mathew said. "He is a teacher."

"Well, that's what Mom always says—that he doesn't have much money. I don't know why."

"I don't know why either," said Mathew. "He couldn't spend a lot on food since he's a vegetarian. Vegetables don't cost a lot."

But it wasn't the right time to reflect on the mysteries of the grown-up world. Mathew could see that Mathilda looked unhappy over the loss of her watch, so he unstrapped his own and offered it to her.

"Here," he said. "You can have mine."

"I don't want yours," she said. "I want my own."

"This one can be yours now."

"But then you won't have one."

"I don't care."

"Well, I do."

They argued amiably, as they usually did, and agreed finally that they would take turns wearing the watch. Today would be Mathilda's turn.

# THIRD BODY FOUND IN PARK

*Police Arrest Homeless Vietnam Vet*

## Angry Parents Storm Mayor's Office

## Police Say Third Body Not Linked With Others

### NEIGHBORHOOD GROUPS WANT HOMELESS OUT OF PARK

## Police Enforce Curfew in Park

Suspect Released in Park Slaying

## Kidnap Attempt at Children's Playground

## *"Park No Longer Safe for Kids," Says PTA President*

## Jogger Describes Assault in Park

## Hysteria Sweeps City

"CLEAN UP PARK," DEMAND CITY HALL DEMONSTRATORS

*HOMELESS MORE FRIGHTENED BY VIGILANTE SPIRIT THAN BY MURDERER ON THE LOOSE*

# Six

UNCLE BEN was not at home.

"Well, naturally," Mathilda said. "This must be the last day of school for him too." She looked down at the Mickey Mouse watch on her wrist. "It's not even twelve yet. He won't be home for another few hours."

Mathew rang the bell again.

"Why are you ringing the bell? I just told you he won't be home."

"I don't know." Mathew looked at all the names and bells on the brass plate. Uncle Ben lived in an apartment house on Fulton Street, right across from the big park in San Francisco. He lived up on the third floor, facing the park, and when you looked out of his window, you could see over some of the trees to more trees. Mathew hadn't been inside his uncle's house for three years, but he remembered looking out of the window and wondering what lay beyond all those tall trees.

He remembered something else as well.

"There's a great hobby store around here somewhere. Remember, Mathilda? After Mom and Uncle Ben had that fight and she made us leave, he called out after us that we should go see the hobby store."

"I don't remember," Mathilda said, "and stop ringing that bell. There's nobody home now. How many times do I have to keep telling you?"

Mathew smiled as he remembered the store. "We were already on the street when Uncle Ben opened his window and called us. Don't you remember? He didn't call Mom because he was angry at her. He called you and me. Mom said not to pay any attention, but we did. We stopped walking and looked up. That's when he said we should go to the hobby store."

Mathilda forgot about Mathew ringing the bell. "Yes, I do remember. That store was on . . . on . . . Geary Boulevard. Mom knew where it was, and after she calmed down, she took us over there."

Mathew took his finger off the bell and nodded. "That's right. First she said no we couldn't go, but we ended up going anyway. I remember I bought a few miniature cars." Mathew shook his head regretfully. "I also remember they had wonderful models of planes, but I wasn't into model planes then."

Now Mathilda was smiling too. "Wasn't I still playing with my old dollhouse then? Yes—I remember. Mom bought me a little piano for the living room and some tiny candlesticks for the dining-room table. I used to love that little house. It's down in the basement now, but I wouldn't mind taking it out again. Jennifer and I used to love playing with it, and even you, Mathew. Remember, you built me some bookcases for the den, and

we made little books out of an old telephone directory?
Do you remember, Mathew?"

Mathew licked his bands. "Why don't we go over
there now? We have a few hours before Uncle Ben
comes home."

"Okay," Mathilda agreed. "It will give us a chance to
look over the neighborhood too. I wonder where our
school will be."

They found the store easily. It was even larger than
they remembered. Mathilda stood, enchanted, in front
of the locked glass case containing the dollhouse furni-
ture. As she inspected the beds, chairs and tables, the
rugs, drapes and chandeliers, all her old enthusiasm for
her little dollhouse returned. It had been over a year
since she'd grown tired of it and packed it away in the
basement.

There was a family of four dolls sitting on a couch in
the living room—a mother, a father, a son and a
daughter. The mother doll was dark-haired and smiling. She wore a yellow flowered dress and high heels.
The father doll was blond and smiling. He wore a suit.
The girl doll was dark-haired and smiling. She wore a
red dress. The boy doll was blond and smiling. He
wore jeans and a checked shirt. They looked very much
like the doll family she had packed away with her little
house, only this family was newer and brighter. Suddenly, Mathilda knew she had to have them. It was silly
to want them so much, but she had to have them.

"How much are they?" she asked the clerk at the
cash register.

"Usually it's twenty dollars for the whole family," the
clerk answered, "but there's a twenty percent end-of-

school sale this week, so you can have them for sixteen dollars."

They're small, Mathilda thought to herself. They won't take up any room at all in Uncle Ben's place. He won't mind. I'm sure he won't mind. But, Mathilda, said a severe voice inside her head that sounded just like her own voice, this is no time to be spending money on toys, is it? No, she answered herself unhappily. No, it isn't. She turned quickly away from the dollhouse family and began looking for Mathew. She found him in the model plane section, a deliriously happy look on his face.

"Just look, Mathilda," he cried, pointing to two huge kits on display. They have the Mercury Redstone and the Crusader Swing-Wing. I've been looking for these two for ages."

"But, Mathew," Mathilda said sternly, "they're very expensive, and they're also very big, and we don't know how much room Uncle Ben will be able to let us have."

Mathew took a deep breath, ran his hand lovingly down one of the kits and said, "Well, maybe another day. It doesn't have to be right now. But they do have the best model collection I've ever seen."

Mathilda watched the smile on his face fade, and she said quickly, "Isn't there something you could buy that would be cheaper and wouldn't take up much room?"

"Well . . ." Mathew had already paused in front of a small, balsa-wood glider. "While we're waiting for Uncle Ben, I guess I could put this little guy together, and maybe fly him out in the park. It's pretty cheap. And small. As a matter of fact, Mathilda, why don't we get two—one for you and one for me?"

"Uh . . . no, thanks, anyway, Mathew, but . . ."

"I'll put it together for you, and then we can race them. We'll get two."

He looked so cheerful that Mathilda just shrugged her shoulders. She guessed she really didn't want that dollhouse family. Not really.

Right across the street from Uncle Ben's apartment house was an old peaked-roof bus shelter. One end opened on the street and the other on the park. Along each side of the shelter there were wooden seats covered with generations and generations of peeling paint. On the ground, cigarette butts, candy wrappers and pigeon droppings mingled.

"There must be a pigeon nest somewhere," Mathew said, looking up into the crisscross beams of the roof.

"There's a pigeon." Mathilda pointed over to the park-side entrance, where a single bird, high up in one of the crossbeams, fluffed its feathers.

"I don't see a nest, though." Mathew walked over to the park entrance and looked up both inside the shelter and out. Then he stepped through it. "Mathilda, come here a minute."

She joined him, and the two of them looked out into a wild, dense world of green trees and bushes. "It's like a jungle here," she said, "and just look back that way."

Both of them turned to look back through the shelter, where the city lay with its cars and buses whizzing by, its people hurrying along and its apartment houses across the street.

"It's like two worlds," Mathew said.

They forgot about the pigeons as they returned to their seats. Mathew started putting the gliders together, and Mathilda tried to remember exactly what the layout of Uncle Ben's apartment was. She couldn't remember if he had two bedrooms or only one.

As soon as Mathew finished putting the gliders together, the twins gathered up their daypacks and went off into the park. They followed the path that led through the bushes to the big central drive. The day was bright and clear, and there was a fresh green smell that made them feel as if they were in the country.

"We're going to love living here, so close to the park," Mathilda said, sniffing the good smells and enjoying the green and yellow sun-drenched world around her. But Mathew was in a hurry to try out the gliders, so he kept moving and Mathilda had to hurry along to keep up with him. After a while they found the wide lawn with its display of flowers in front of the hothouses. They dropped their daypacks on the ground, sailed their gliders off in the air and darted here and there, following in their path.

Suddenly, Mathilda experienced a strange and unfamiliar sensation. "Mathew!" she called. "Mathew!"

But his glider had disappeared behind a clump of yellow flowers, and it took him some time to respond. "What?"

"I'm hungry."

"Hungry?"

Mathew looked down at his wrist for his watch, but Mathilda was wearing it. "What time is it?"

"A quarter after two. I'm really hungry. Aren't you?"

Mathew didn't think he was hungry. He seldom was. But he did feel something unfamiliar. Usually by a quarter after two, he had eaten his lunch.

"Let's go get something to eat," Mathilda suggested.

"But shouldn't we stay close to Uncle Ben's house?"

"He won't be home until after three. Let's grab a hot dog. We can be back before that."

They found a stand behind the Music Concourse, and both twins had hot dogs and Cokes. Mathew was surprised at how good they tasted. Generally he didn't notice.

They were back in the shelter by ten to three, and now they stayed either inside the shelter, watching the house, or walking back and forth in front of it.

At four o'clock, Mathilda said, "Maybe he came back earlier. Maybe school let out earlier. Maybe I should go and ring his bell just in case he got home while we were eating lunch."

"I'll go," Mathew said. He enjoyed ringing his uncle's bell and looking at the whole panel of bells and names.

"We'll both go." The twins crossed the street, and Mathew rang the bell several times. Nobody answered. They hung around in front of the house for a while and then crossed the street again and returned to the shelter. Two men were now sitting there, smoking. Both of them wore old army jackets, and one had a scarf wrapped around his forehead. The one without the scarf began coughing.

"Stop it!" the other one said. "You're driving me crazy."

The twins sat as far away as they could, on the other side from the men, and tried not to look at them.

The coughing continued, and the other man began yelling, "Will you cut that out? God damn it, you never stop."

The coughing man stopped finally and said in a

raspy voice, "I'm not doing it on purpose, you know."

"What time is it now?" Mathew asked in a low voice.

"Four thirty," she whispered.

"He should be here soon," Mathew said.

The twins moved closer together and looked very hard through the opening on the city side across the street to their uncle's house.

"Hey, kid!" one of the men called out.

The twins kept looking out of the opening.

"I said, 'Hey, kid!' " the voice repeated, only louder.

Mathew was frightened, but he turned his head carefully towards the men and said, "Uh, what?"

"Not you. The other one—the girl—you!"

Mathilda moved so close to Mathew she was practically sitting on him. "What?" she asked.

"What time is it?" the man with the scarf demanded.

"Uh—four thirty," she answered.

"Let's go see if he's home, Mathilda," Mathew said, getting up quickly and pulling on her arm.

"Come over here a minute, kid," said the man with the scarf.

"We have to go now," Mathew said.

"I want to see your watch. Come over here," the man insisted.

They should have run. They both knew it, but they were also used to obeying when a grown-up told them to do something. Slowly, they moved towards him.

"Let's see it," said the man, holding out his arm.

Mathilda held hers out, and he took it and looked down at the watch. "It's a Mickey Mouse watch," he said, bending over it.

"We each got one for Christmas," Mathilda said,

looking down at the man's thin brown hair, and the patches of scalp that showed through underneath.

"A Mickey Mouse watch," he repeated. "Look at it, Al."

Mathilda wanted to pull her arm away and run, but she stood there as the other man came closer and also bent over her arm. Now she could smell something. Not the clean, fresh smell of the leaves and the grass out in the park, but a smell she wasn't used to. A smell she didn't like.

The man with the scarf began laughing. "I had one once, just like this, only the band was black." He looked up into Mathilda's face. He was smiling and a couple of teeth were missing. Mathilda noticed that his thin hair was long and gathered into a ponytail. "I really loved that watch," he said.

"Well, we've got to be going," Mathew said, tugging at Mathilda's arm. "It was real nice talking to you, but we're in kind of a hurry."

"I never had a Mickey Mouse watch," said the other man, the one who smelled bad. There were greasy patches on his jacket, Mathilda noticed, and a big green stain on his cheek.

"You have to be careful not to wind it too much," the man with the scarf said, letting go of Mathilda's arm. "If you wind it too much, you'll break it. That's what happened to mine."

The other man started coughing again, and Mathilda said quickly, "I'll be careful. Thanks a lot." She and Mathew hurried out of the shelter and across the street.

"I think they're looking at us," she said.

"Just keep walking and don't look back," he told her.

They walked quickly to the corner, turned it and ran.

They ran for a couple of blocks and then, completely out of breath, they stopped and leaned against the side of a building, gasping.

"I thought they were going to steal the watch," Mathilda said.

"So did I, at first. But then I thought they weren't going to steal it. They were kind of weird, but I don't think they were bad."

"They smelled bad," Mathilda said. "Especially the one who coughed." She held her nose, and then they both began to laugh.

"Look—why don't we call Uncle Ben," Mathew suggested. "I don't want to go back to the shelter, and I don't want to stand in front of Uncle Ben's house."

"Maybe they won't be there," Mathilda said. "Maybe they're just waiting for a bus."

"Well, let's not go back yet. We can try to call him first anyway."

They found a phone booth and looked up their uncle in the directory. There was his name, Benjamin M. Burns, his address and his phone number.

"Let me call him," Mathilda said.

"No, let me."

They argued for a while and then chose. Mathilda won. She dialed the number, and Mathew told her to hold up the phone so he could hear too. They both heard the phone ring once, twice, three times, four times, and then their uncle's voice.

"Hello," said the voice. "This is Ben. I'm sorry I cannot come to the phone right now, but if you'll leave a message and your phone number at the sound of the beep, I'll return your call as soon as I can."

# Seven

As the darkness spread, the shelter emptied, and Mathew and Mathilda, tired from walking up and down in front of Uncle Ben's house, crossed the street and gratefully sat down inside.

"He's probably out late with some of his friends," Mathilda repeated for the twentieth or twenty-first time. "We can watch for him from here."

She fell asleep first. Her head rolled around at first but finally settled back against the wall. Mathew tried to stay awake, but when it grew completely dark, he fell asleep too.

Mathilda was dreaming about a toasted cheese sandwich, a smoking-hot toasted cheese sandwich, when she heard the sirens and snapped awake. "Police!" she cried as she shook Mathew's arm. "Maybe they're looking for us." She pulled him up, and the two of them ran through the shelter, and out into the park. There were others in the shelter—she saw outlines of bodies, stretched out on the ground, sitting on benches, standing and smoking in corners, and she could hear the sound of breathing and coughing.

"What? What?" Mathew cried, still asleep, unsure of where he was, cold and beginning to feel terrified.

"Shh! Shh!" Mathilda said, pulling him into a space between some dark bushes. "It's the police. Maybe they're looking for us. Shh!"

The two of them huddled, shivering, up against a big tree, and listened. They heard voices at first, some complaining and whining, "Aw, can't you leave us alone for a change? Just for tonight?" Others, loud and commanding, "Move along . . . can't stay here . . . get up now . . . Get up!"

Mathew whimpered softly, and Mathilda pressed his arm to get him to shut up. But his teeth began chattering, and his headgear felt icy cold.

The whining voices were closer now. "Give us a break . . . no place to go . . ."

Rustling sounds. Thumps. Bumps. Movement near their bushes. A man's voice saying, "Lousy cops!" Somebody coughing . . . a child crying.

"Mathilda!" Mathew began, but she put her hand over his mouth, and they stayed there silently until the movement around them stopped. They fell asleep again, leaning together against the tree. Mathilda heard, inside her sleep, whispering voices that said, "Go home! Go home!"

It was still dark when they both woke up. It was dark, but there was a ripple of comfort in the air that made them feel the day was near. Neither of them spoke. They both rose and tried to shake off the cold ache in their bodies. It was still dark, but they could see, not ten feet away, an old woman covered with cardboard, fast asleep.

Mathew took Mathilda's hand and pulled her carefully out of the bushes. They had to pass through the shelter. An old man sat there sleeping, and a teenage girl in a sleeping bag lay stretched out on the ground, her eyes wide-open. They passed her, but she said nothing.

"He must be home by now," Mathew said as they crossed the street. He rang the bell, and the two of them waited for the buzzer. He kept ringing the bell.

Finally Mathilda said, "Let me do it." She rang and rang, but nobody answered.

"Maybe he's asleep," Mathew said.

"Maybe he didn't come home," Mathilda answered.

Mathew could not shake off the cold. It lay on his shivering feet, and he felt it spreading back and forth from his headgear to the bands on his teeth. "Mathilda . . ." he began, but then he shook his head and stamped his feet. No! he thought to himself. No!

"I have to go," Mathilda said, hopping from one foot to the other.

Both of them looked across the street to the shelter. The teenage girl was gone, but the old man still sat there, sleeping.

"I don't want to go back through there," Mathilda said.

A pale light began moving across the sky. "What time is it?" Mathew asked.

Mathilda looked at the watch. "Five thirty," she said. Then she took it off her wrist and handed it to him. "It's your turn now," she said, "but I have to go real bad."

Mathew strapped his watch back on his wrist, and suddenly he was himself again. He looked across the street and pointed to another entrance to the park, only about a block away.

"Let's go," she said. "Fast!"

They hurried down the street and crossed it into the park, past the stone posts topped with crouching, snarling, stone wildcats who kept silent guard. Each of the twins disappeared behind a bush and soon, feeling more comfortable and not quite so cold, they moved out into the big open drive. Mathilda pointed to the first bench they found. "Sit down," she said. "We have to talk."

There were leaves in her brother's hair, she noticed, and the white collar of his red and white polo shirt was no longer white. "We could go home," she said.

Mathew licked his bands miserably. "No," he said in a small voice. But he meant no.

Mathilda nodded. "Okay. Then maybe we should go someplace else."

"Where?"

"That's the problem. I don't know where."

"Why don't we wait?" Mathew said. "He probably just slept over at a friend's."

"I bet he did," Mathilda agreed. "He'll probably be home soon."

"But maybe he'll be away for the weekend."

Across the road, they watched an old man stop in front of a trash can and begin to rummage around inside. They saw him pull out three empty cans and put them into a shopping bag he was carrying.

"I guess he's going to bring them into a recycling

center," Mathew said, remembering the time all the kids in his school cleaned up the neighborhood.

They watched as he opened a paper bag and pulled something out. He held it up in front of his face, smelled it and then put it into his mouth.

"Yuk!" Mathilda said. "Did you see that? Did you see what he just did? He's eating garbage. He must be crazy."

"I don't want to stay in that shelter anymore," Mathew said. "If Uncle Ben's gone for the weekend, we might have to stay out another night. I don't want to stay there."

"Me neither," Mathilda said, watching the old man open another bag and pull out what looked like a half-eaten banana. "Let's go." She jumped up.

"Let's go where?"

"Let's just go."

They hurried along Kennedy Drive as the pale gray light in the sky turned to white. The twins had been to Golden Gate Park before, but always with one or both parents. Those times, they had half noticed other families like themselves, picnicking on the grass, coming and going to and from the museum, laughing, arguing, tossing Frisbees around. They had seen joggers in bright colors, bikers and softball teams in school uniforms. Sometimes they had come to puppet shows or Shakespeare in the park, and had joined other people like themselves spread out confidently on the green lawns.

Now in the dim light of dawn, they found others in the park, but nobody looked like the people they had seen in the bright daylight. A child was crying—they couldn't see it as they hurried along the drive, but they heard it—a thin, jagged cry like that of a very young baby. It came from behind a clump of trees near the museum. They heard a woman's voice talking to it, and two other children, younger than themselves, sat on a low wall, silently watching them as they went by. They saw an old woman, dressed in a long, torn skirt, barefoot, with blue swollen feet, sitting on a path, talking to herself. They noticed another man sleeping on a bench, and Mathilda said, "Who are all these people? What are they doing here?"

Mathew said, "I think there's a big lake around here. They have a refreshment stand. We can get something to eat."

As soon as he said it, he realized that he was hungry. And that it was a strange and exciting feeling.

"It's up this way, Mathilda. I remember from the last time we were here and Dad took us rowing."

They turned off Kennedy Drive and went up the path that lead to the lake. They passed the statue of Pioneer Mother and giggled over her two naked children, passed the little log cabin in the glen and came at last to the big lake just as the day broke over it.

The refreshment stand was closed.

Mathew looked at his watch impatiently. It was only six fifteen. "I guess the stand won't open until later," he said unhappily.

Mathilda looked out over the boats tied up at the small pier. "I wish we could take a boat out," she said.

"Maybe we can later," Mathew said.

They began to circle the lake, watching the ducks and geese furrowing the waters as they swam. When they came to the Roman Bridge, leading to Strawberry Island in the center of the lake, they crossed over.

As soon as they did, Mathilda said, "Listen!"

Mathew listened. "I don't hear anything," he said.

But Mathilda was hurrying along the path that circled the island at its base. He followed her, and then he heard it too. Before he saw it, he heard the sound of a waterfall. Mathilda was already pulling off her clothes when he arrived.

"Come on, Mathew," she cried. "Let's get under it."

Mathew looked up at the falls tumbling down from the top of Strawberry Hill. "It's cold," he said, "and the water is dirty."

Mathilda was already splashing around underneath it, yelling for him to come on in. Reluctantly, he pulled off his clothes and joined her.

It was cold, and the pool of water they stood in was green and murky, but as they leaped around inside and splashed each other, he forgot to notice that his teeth were chattering and the rest of him was shivering in the cool morning air.

They dried themselves off with leaves and then put their clothes back on again. The sun was out when they came to a bright red and green Chinese pavilion with a tiled roof that was caving in. Around it was a wire-mesh fence and signs that said DANGER and KEEP OUT.

"Let's climb over," Mathilda said.

Mathew pointed to the signs, but Mathilda was already halfway up the fence. He began climbing too. He wasn't as nimble as his sister, and she had to give him a hand. But once over, he knew.

"Here's where we'll stay tonight," he said.

The twins walked down the little stone path and up the stairs into the pavilion. It was open on all sides, and in the center was a black marble table with white marble stools around it.

"We'll sleep here tonight," he repeated. Then he looked around the floor of the pavilion and poked around the bushes surrounding it. "We'll come back later, after the park closes, when nobody's around. We'll be safe here."

"I wish I'd brought my flashlight," Mathilda said.

"We can manage without one."

"And I was freezing last night. Too bad we didn't bring our sleeping bags."

"It's only going to be for another night," Mathew said. "If he doesn't come home today, I mean. Maybe he'll come home soon. Meanwhile, we'll just keep on calling. Maybe we should leave a message on his machine, just in case he accesses it."

"No!" Mathilda shook her head. "That's too risky. If somebody else takes his messages, they'd know where we are."

The twins circled the island, exploring their new home. They found another bridge, a pretty, old-fashioned stone bridge that had the date 1893 carved on it, and they crossed back again to the mainland. Two women joggers in bright reds and greens flashed by them, a teenage boy on a bike . . . familiar-looking people populating a familiar daylight world.

"Maybe the refreshment stand is open now," Mathew said, looking at his watch. "It's ten after eight. Maybe they open early on Saturday."

They passed a woman walking a dog, who smiled at them and wished them good morning.

In front of the refreshment stand, a woman sat on a bench nursing a baby. The two small children who had looked silently at Mathew and Mathilda a couple of hours earlier were fiddling_around with the popcorn machine in front of the closed stand—sticking their fingers up into its interior and licking them.

Apart from them, maybe twenty feet away, stood a daylight person, an old woman dressed in neat daylight clothes, feeding a group of ducks and geese that had climbed out of the lake and stood clustered around her. "Here you are, Henry," she said to one gray-headed goose, holding out a piece of bread to him. "No, no, Marjorie, don't be rude," she told a stately white one who had just nipped her neighbor. "There's plenty for everybody."

One of the children, tired of the empty popcorn machine, moved over towards her and stood silently watching—his eyes not on the feeding ducks and geese but on the bread in her hand. The other one also left the popcorn machine and began digging inside a trash bin right behind where the old woman stood.

"Look, Kevin, look," he cried out to his brother, unwrapping the remains of a hot dog in a bun and holding it up to him. His brother's eyes remained fixed on the bread in the old woman's hands. Suddenly, from around the side of the refreshment stand, a huge, snarling man burst out.

"God-damned little creep, I've told you before to stay away from there." He hurled himself at the child, who shrank from the trash bin and fled towards the old woman. Kicking away viciously at the ducks and geese that squawked and cackled in terror, the man followed the little boy, his great arms outstretched.

The child's mother, feeding her baby, stood up and began screeching. But the child, terror struck, reached out to the old woman and clung to her skirts.

"I'll tear you apart," roared the man, nearly upon him, but the old woman turned to face the man, and the child shrank behind her.

"Get out of my way," howled the man, trying to reach behind her.

Even from where the twins stood, they could see tears in the old woman's eyes. "How can you . . . how can you . . . be . . . so cruel?" she cried in a sweet, thin, high voice.

"I'm hungry, lady," roared the man. "Do you know what that means? Hungry? I'm hungrier than those ducks you keep feeding. How about feeding me?"

He reached out again. Whether it was for her purse or the child cowering behind her, the twins could not determine, because now the mother was upon him, her baby in her arms. Shrieking and clawing, she reached up with one hand, and the twins could see the bright red path of her fingernails on his cheek.

With a roar, he struck out at her, and she fell to the ground, scattering some of the geese, the baby still in her arms. The old woman quickly opened her purse and handed him a couple of bills. "Go away!" she said. "Go away!"

The man waved the bills in the air. "I'm warning you, all of you," he howled. "Stay out of my way. And keep those brats out of my places, or I'll get you all."

"Go! Please go!" the old woman cried, the child's face still buried in her skirts. His brother, the younger child, managed to pick up a large piece of bread she had dropped and began gobbling it up.

The man put a hand up to his bruised face and kicked at the dark-headed goose named Henry before turning and moving off.

## ALL POINTS ALERT

# KIDNAPPED

A brother and sister, twins, were apparently kidnapped last Friday on their way to school. . . .

## Distraught Parents Offer Reward $$$

## TWINS DISAPPEAR WITHOUT A TRACE

BOY WITH HEADBAND SEEN IN SAN DIEGO. OTHER WITNESSES REPORT SEEING BOY WITH HEADBAND IN LAS VEGAS AND FRESNO.

## Man Arrested for Eating Rare Plants in Park

**Description of Missing Twins**
Boy and girl, 11 years old. Boy: dark blond hair, blue eyes, headgear, wearing jeans, red-and-white striped shirt. Girl: dark brown hair and eyes, wearing jeans, pink shirt

## Drop in Number of Visitors to Golden Gate Park

## "Find Our Children," Tearful Mother Pleads

# Eight

"MATHEW," MATHILDA YELPED, "did you mail that card?"

"Of course I did," Mathew said. "Just before we got on the bus. Didn't you see me?"

The twins were wandering the streets around Uncle Ben's house early Sunday morning. They had each rung his bell several times, and Mathilda had dialed his number from the phone on the corner and held up the phone so that they both could listen to Uncle Ben's voice say, "Hello. This is Ben. I'm sorry I cannot come to the phone right now, but if you'll leave a message and your phone number at the sound of the beep, I'll return your call as soon as I can."

The Sunday papers lay in a heap on the sidewalk, and under the big "Kidnapped" headlines were pictures of each of them.

"That was my class picture last year," Mathew said. "I don't look like that anymore."

"But mine is from this year," Mathilda said. "Isn't

that funny that they used mine from this year and yours from last year?"

The twins discussed it for a few moments before returning to the important question. "Are you sure you mailed the card? I don't remember seeing you."

"I know I mailed it. I remember looking at the pickup time, and it said four o'clock."

"Well, why wouldn't they have received it yesterday then?"

"Sometimes the mail is late. They'll certainly get it tomorrow."

Mathilda read the story under the picture, and then she looked down at the pink shirt she was wearing and over at the red-and-white striped shirt Mathew was wearing.

"We're going to have to get some new clothes," she said. "Look here. It says I'm wearing a pink shirt and you're wearing a red-and-white striped shirt. We only brought one shirt and our sweaters. Let's put on our sweaters."

They pulled their sweaters out of their daypacks and put them on. Then both of them read the rest of the description. "Mathew," Mathilda said, "you have to stop wearing that headgear. And can you remove the wire bands from your teeth?"

"Yes!" Mathew said. "Yes, I can." He unhooked the headgear, which he had continued to wear ever since he left home and began heading towards the trash can at the corner.

"No!" Mathilda said. "No! Don't throw it out. If somebody finds it, they might figure out where we are."

"I'll get the bands off later," Mathew said happily. "I

just have to twist a few wires, and then the whole thing will come off. And you know something, Mathilda?"

"What?"

"I'm never going to wear bands again. No matter what happens. I'm going to say no."

Mathilda read on. "Brother and sister," she mumbled. "Twins."

"Even if Uncle Ben wants me to wear them," Mathew said, "I won't."

"Mathew," Mathilda said, looking at him with her head cocked to one side, "would you like to be a girl?"

"No," Mathew said. "I mean you're okay, and so is Mom—most of the time. But I'm satisfied being a boy. What about you? Would you like to be a boy?"

"No," Mathilda said. "But one of us is going to have to change." She pointed to the words *brother and sister, boy and girl* in the article. "At least for today, or until Uncle Ben comes home."

"I don't look like a girl," Mathew said.

"Well, I don't look like a boy."

Each of them inspected the other, and Mathew finally said, "You could look like a boy. Your hair is short, and if you got another shirt . . ."

"No," said Mathilda, "you could get another shirt too. You'd look like a girl if you wore a pink—no, not pink—maybe a shirt with yellow and green flowers."

"I don't want to wear a shirt with yellow and green flowers."

"Well, I don't want to wear a boy's shirt, either."

The situation was deadlocked, but then Mathew used the one powerful argument he had. "You could change your name."

"What?"

"Well, if you had to be a boy, you couldn't be Mathilda, could you?"

"No. But you can't be Mathew anymore, even if you
go on being a boy. Besides, I want to change my name
to a girl's name, not a boy's name."

"Suppose I let you pick both of our new names,"
Mathew said slyly. "What about that?"

"You mean you'd let me give you a new name too?"

"Yes. If you change to a boy, then I'll let you give us
both new names. But if I have to be a girl, I'll call myself something terrible. Something worse than Mathilda."

"Nothing is worse than Mathilda."

"Oh, yes. There are lots of names worse than Mathilda."

"Name one."

"Well, how about . . . how about . . . "

The twins continued walking along, talking and arguing as the sun rose and the little shops along the streets
began opening. Daylight people suddenly appeared—
getting into cars, sweeping streets, carrying bags of
food.

"Rosemary is worse than Mathilda."

"No it isn't."

"Gertrude. There. Gertrude is worse than Mathilda."
Mathilda remained silent.

"You even said so," Mathew said. "And what about
Mildred or Loretta?"

"Loretta's not so bad."

Mathew could hear his sister's voice growing
thoughtful and knew victory was near.

"What do you think of my name, of Mathew?" he
pressed on. "Do you like my name?"

"Not particularly," she said. "I like plain names for boys, like Ben or Bob or Bill. I like Bill a lot."

"Well, you can be Bill," he said. "How about that? I could even call you Billy."

"Billy," she said softly. "I like that."

"And I could be Bob."

"No. No," Mathilda insisted. "Not Bob. That's too close to Billy. You have to be something different, so nobody will think we're twins. Let me see. How about John, for instance? How would you like to be John?"

"No," Mathew said firmly. "I would not like to be John. There's this kid in my class, John Young. He's always playing jokes on other kids, and once he knocked my Ram Jet model off my desk. He said it was an accident. No, I don't want to be John."

"Well, you said"—Mathilda grinned her cruel smile—"that I could name you anything I liked."

"Anything but John. You wouldn't make me be John, Mathilda. You wouldn't be that mean."

"Well, if you make me be a boy, then you have to be John."

They argued all the way over to the bagel bakery on Geary Boulevard and then stopped outside, sniffing the good fresh-bread smells.

"I'm hungry," Mathew said. "Lately, I'm always hungry."

"How much money have you got left?" Mathilda asked.

Mathew pulled the money out of his pocket. "Twenty-four dollars and thirty cents. What about you?"

"Eighteen dollars and twelve cents."

"Well, that's okay," said Mathew. "Uncle Ben will

probably be home tonight. I guess he's just gone for the weekend. Right?"

Mathilda hesitated. "Probably," she said, "but suppose . . ."

Mathew shook his head. "I'm starving," he said. "I'll go in and get us some bagels. You'd better wait out here. Until you become a boy, we'd better keep you out of sight."

Mathilda watched Mathew enter the store. It was already full of people, and she moved away to one side and began thinking again of names. Yes, she'd be Billy. She started humming, "Oh, where have you been, Billy Boy, Billy Boy? Oh, where have you been, charming Billy?"

Yes, she liked the name Billy just fine, but how about Mathew? Was he going to be John? If she had to be a boy, then it was only fair that he should be John. Still— if he really hated the name . . . She had always hated her name, and she didn't really want him to be unhappy. . . .

Mathew finally emerged with a bag of warm bagels. How wonderful they smelled!

"I got a bunch of different ones," he said. "There's onion, garlic, poppyseed and raisin."

"I'll take a raisin," Mathilda said.

Mathew handed her one. He took an onion, and they continued walking without speaking as they took large, hungry bites out of the delicious, warm bagels.

"How about Charlie or Jim?" Mathilda asked, her mouth full.

"What?"

Mathilda swallowed. "How about Charlie or Jim?

And that's final. You can choose either one of those two names. And now, I'll have a poppyseed bagel."

Mathew chose Charlie, and by the time they had finished their bagels, it was time to make the transformation.

And it was easy. That Sunday morning, at a number of the houses they passed, people were having garage sales. They bought two boys' shirts for Mathilda—one was orange and black and said San Francisco Giants on it, and the other was just a plain blue-and-green striped boy's jersey shirt with a stain on one sleeve. They paid seventy-five cents for both shirts and one dollar for two new shirts for Mathew. His were just ordinary boys' shirts—one solid blue and the other green-and-white striped.

"I was cold last night," Mathilda said, looking at an old sleeping bag for seven dollars, "but, of course, if Uncle Ben comes back by today or tomorrow, I guess I could manage another night."

"We can pile some more leaves over us tonight," Mathew said. "Last night was a lot better than the night before, wasn't it?"

Mathilda nodded. Yes, last night had been a lot better. They had hung around the lake all day yesterday, eating hot dogs and popcorn, and when everybody had gone home, they had crossed the Roman Bridge, followed the trail to the Chinese pavilion and climbed over the fence. Mathew had dragged branches from the bushes around the lake to make a mattress for them, and as the night grew colder, they had used the branches as blankets.

It had been calm and peaceful on their little island.

There were none of the night noises, and they had seen none of the night people, as they had the night before. They had slept deeply and well, with the sound of the waterfall in their ears. In the morning, even though they were cold and hungry, they had still taken a morning bath under the falls.

"Let's buy a towel," Mathew said, picking up a frayed, faded blue one that was marked twenty cents.

"Let's buy two," Mathilda said recklessly, "and then we'd better go someplace where I can change."

Mathilda the girl became Billy the boy about an hour afterwards, up above their Chinese pavilion at the top of Strawberry Hill. There was nobody up there, so she pulled off her pink shirt and put on the San Francisco Giants shirt. Then she smoothed her hair and said, "You have to change your shirt too, Charlie, and get those bands off your teeth. Right away."

"Okay, Billy," Mathew said. He put on the new old blue shirt and then said, "We'd better bury them."

"You're right," Mathilda said. "If we throw them out, somebody might find them. But what will we make a hole with? We don't have shovels."

Mathew handed her a stick and found another one for himself. They buried the shirts in a dense part of the underbrush on the side of the hill. Soon the two of them were sitting on the top of the hill, looking down at the lake below. It was a pleasant, peaceful scene with daylight people engaged in daylight activities. Somebody familiar was handing food over to the crazy, wild man they had seen yesterday, and Mathew noticed how even he seemed peaceful and pleasant.

"It's not so hard being a boy," Mathilda said. "All I

had to do was change my shirt. You could have done the same thing, and you would have been a girl."

"Let's take a boat out today," Mathew said, pointing down to the little boats already passing to and fro on the lake.

"Do you think we should?" Mathilda said sensibly. "I mean, just in case he doesn't come back tonight."

"Oh, he'll come back tonight—or tomorrow," Mathew said. He was fiddling with a wire inside his mouth as he talked, twisting it and turning it until it broke and the bands on his teeth came off. "There," he said. "There."

"Let's go." Mathilda jumped up and pulled him up too. Then the two of them went running down the stairs on the side of the waterfall, hurried across the bridge and ended up at the boathouse.

"Wait a minute," Mathilda said. "I have to go."

"Me too," said Mathew.

They walked around to the back of the building where the women's and men's rooms were. Mathilda headed for the women's room and Mathew for the men's room. But just before the entrance, Mathilda hesitated and looked back nervously at Mathew. He had paused and was grinning at her.

"No," she yelled out. "No, I won't."

"Come on, Billy," Mathew said. "The men's room is over here. Not there. Come on now."

So she went. It really wasn't as easy changing into a boy as she had thought.

"Anybody could have done it," the policeman said, looking down at the new body. "Everybody hated him."

He lay in a clump of lilies of the Nile. The impact of his large body had broken some of the delicate necks of the flowers, and several spidery blue blossoms were scattered across his chest.

The policewoman pointed to the scratch marks on his face. "We'll try to find the woman who did that to him. We've gotten a good description from a couple of witnesses."

"But everybody hated him," said the policeman. "He claimed all the trash cans around the lake as his own property. You know that. There wasn't one homeless person who didn't hate him."

"And then he had that big fistfight with Caruso, and two nights ago he even tried to choke poor Marbles. . . ." The policewoman looked down at the dead body with distaste. "Nobody was safe from him—women, children, dogs, cats, birds. . . . They say he killed any bird or animal he could lay his hands on and ate it."

"I know," said the policeman, shaking his head. "To tell you the truth, I always thought he was the killer."

"Me too," the policewoman said. "We'll just have to start all over again. But I want that woman picked up for questioning."

"If we can find her," said the policeman. "Meanwhile, I have a new plan. . . ."

# Nine

"WHAT DO YOU BOYS want?" the woman demanded. "Why do you keep hanging around here, ringing the bells?"

"We're only ringing our—uh—uh—Ben Burns' bell. We're not ringing anybody else's," Mathilda said, trying to make her voice sound like a boy's.

The woman hardly listened to her. She was a sharp-faced woman dressed in old clothes, and she stood in the doorway with an angry, suspicious look on her face.

Mathew looked past her into the dimly lit hall. If only the two of them could get into the building, he thought, maybe they could just stay inside until Uncle Ben returned. He was sure to return today, Monday.

"Uh . . . maybe the bell is broken," he said. "Maybe we could just go upstairs to his apartment and knock on his door."

The woman moved out of the doorway, letting the door close behind her. "Who are you kids, anyway?"

she asked, her mouth tight and angry. "What do you want him for?"

"Oh—we're just . . . uh . . . friends," Mathilda said.

The woman moved so close, she was almost touching them. "You kids in his class? You trying to play some trick on him?"

"Oh, no," Mathew said. "We just want to . . . to . . . ask him a question."

"You're trying to sell him something, aren't you?"

"Oh, no!"

"Bug off!" the woman said, making a pushing motion with her hands.

"Maybe we could just leave a note in his mailbox?" Mathilda said desperately.

The woman reached out for her, making what sounded like a snarling sound, and Mathilda went flying off, across the street, Mathew right behind her.

"Who do you think *that* was?" Mathilda asked, once they were safely back inside the park.

"Maybe the custodian. But why wouldn't she let us put a note in Uncle Ben's mailbox?"

"I don't know. We can't write a letter because we don't want anybody to see the postmark."

"Why don't we try leaving a message on his answering machine?" Mathew said.

"No. Just in case somebody is taking his messages."

"Well, then it wouldn't be a good idea to leave a note in his mailbox either. But we've got to get in touch with him."

"I'm getting worried," Mathilda said. "Where is he anyway?"

"Maybe something is wrong." Mathew spoke slowly.

"Maybe he's upstairs in his apartment, sick, or . . . I didn't like that woman. There's something suspicious about her."

Mathilda was thinking. "If he was upstairs, sick, or . . . something else, he wouldn't be able to pick up his mail, right?"

"Right."

"Okay. Then his mailbox would be full of mail. I've got an idea. Later tonight, one of us should go back and ring his bell and also look in his mailbox. If it's full of mail, then we'd know something is wrong, and we'd have to . . ."

"Have to what?"

"Call the police," she said, "and tell them."

The day turned very warm. Suddenly all of summer's foggy breezes dissolved. By midafternoon it was hot, and it stayed hot even when darkness came.

Mathew insisted on going alone. So Mathilda stood across the street—not inside the shelter, but directly across the street—and watched. She saw her brother approach Uncle Ben's house cautiously, look around carefully and then ring the bell, ring it again and again. She saw him bend over to peer into Uncle Ben's mailbox, turn, look towards her and shake his head. No. No mail inside the box. So where was Uncle Ben?

That night, for the first time since they began sleeping out in the park, Mathew and Mathilda were not cold. They lay on their mattress of leaves and branches and slept without shivering. Mathilda dreamed of birds singing in a tropical forest and woke up in the early daylight to hear a man singing and see a man's face pressed up against the outside of the fence, watching her.

"Mathew! Mathew!" she whispered. "Wake up!"

The man nodded and smiled at her and continued singing. His voice sounded familiar. Her friend Jennifer's mother loved opera and always played records of people singing the way the man was singing. But it was always during the day and never out of doors in the pale light of dawn with the sound of the waterfall behind them.

Mathew sat up. "What should we do?" he whispered.

The man pulled his face away from the fence, took a very deep breath, raised his head high in the air and concluded his song on a very loud, ringing note.

"Will you shut up, Caruso?" a sleepy voice shouted from across the lake. "It's not even morning yet."

"If he climbs over the fence," Mathilda whispered, "we can jump in the lake and swim across."

The man put his face up against the fence and smiled. Even in the pale light, the twins could see that his cheeks were red from the exertions of his song. "That really used to wow them in La Scala," he said.

"Uh, what was that?" Mathew asked.

"La Scala. The opera house in Milan. I used to sing there. My name is Victor Minetta. Now you know who I am."

"We don't know much about opera," Mathilda said and then added quickly, "but it really sounded nice."

"Around here," the man said scornfully, "they call me Caruso. But my voice is better than Caruso's. He didn't have taste. I was known for my taste."

"It really sounded nice," Mathilda repeated feebly.

"Who are you, please?" the man asked, smiling graciously.

"We're—uh—friends," Mathew said. "This is—uh—Billy, and I'm Charlie."

"My father's name was Charles," Caruso told them. "He had a beautiful tenor voice too. Would you like to hear his favorite song? It's 'Che Gelida Manina' from *La Bohème.*"

"Thank you very much," Mathew said, "but . . ."

Caruso stepped back from the fence, took a deep breath and began singing.

"He sure can sing loud," Mathilda whispered.

Now there were other voices from across the lake, yelling at him to shut up. Somebody threw a rock, and somebody else a stick.

But Caruso finished his song with one ear-splitting peal, bowed to the children and trotted off down the path.

"I guess we'd better find some other place to sleep tonight," Mathilda said regretfully. "Now that he knows we're here, I mean. We'll have to find a place that's more secluded."

"I think we're safest here," Mathew said. "Anybody who was after us would have to first climb over the fence, and if that happened, we could jump in the lake and swim across."

"But suppose they came from the lake?" Mathilda pointed through the bushes to the one side of the pavilion that was open.

"We'd hear them," said Mathew, "and then we could climb over the fence."

They kept on discussing it even as they took their morning bath under the waterfalls. Mathilda said she would feel safer if they found another sleeping place. Mathew insisted they were safest inside the pavilion.

"We're forgetting all about Uncle Ben," Mathilda said as they used their new frayed towels to dry themselves off. "Maybe he came home last night."

"Oh, that's right," Mathew said vaguely. "Uncle Ben. I did forget."

"How could you?" Mathilda looked intently at her brother. "It's awful having to stay here, isn't it? Aren't you anxious for him to come home?"

"I guess so," Mathew said, "but I was just thinking how I could fix the roof of the pavilion to stop the tiles from falling off. Anyway, let's see if we can hide our daypacks in the bushes today. I hate to have to keep carrying all our stuff with us."

"I want to call Uncle Ben," Mathilda said. "As soon as we straighten up, I want to call him. We can use the phone near the boathouse."

They tidied up the pavilion, moving all the leaves and branches off to the bushes and hiding their daypacks there as well. By the time they reached the boathouse, the day had turned hot. The old woman who fed the ducks and geese was already out, providing breakfast to all her friends who gathered around her, honking and quacking. "Here's a nice piece of zwieback for you, Henry," she said, feeding the gray-headed goose a large crunchy piece of toast, which suddenly looked very appetizing to Mathew. "Marjorie . . . Dolores . . . try a piece of Maud's angel cake. I baked it just for you." She offered each of the two stately white ducks a piece of what looked like a delicate, pale foamy cake from out of a large plastic bag she held.

"Oh, yum," Mathew said. "I bet that tastes good."

A little boy came running out from one side of the boathouse. He threw his arms around the woman's legs and, reaching into her plastic bag, pulled out a large piece of cake and began eating it.

The old woman rested her hand on his head and said softly, "I wondered where you were. I haven't seen you and the rest of your family for a few days. Where is your mother?"

The child—he must have been about four or five—reached back into the bag for another piece of the cake.

"Where is your mother, dear?" the old woman repeated, turning his face gently up to hers. "Just tell me that."

"No," said the boy, his mouth full of cake, reaching back into the sack.

The old woman shook her head sadly. "This isn't a good breakfast for you, dear. Your mother should look after you better. I want to speak to her. Just tell Maud where she is."

"Let's go call Uncle Ben," said Mathilda, watching the supply of bread and cake diminish as the child gobbled down another piece of the angel cake.

They walked around to the back of the boathouse and found a man and woman standing in front of the phone booth. They were both dressed in dirty jeans, and torn flannel shirts. The woman's mouth was cut and bleeding. As they drew closer, the man reached over and slapped the woman's face so hard her head snapped back and she began crying.

"I haven't got any more money," she sobbed. "You know I don't."

"You do, you witch—you always have money. You've got it on you someplace. Now you'd better . . ."

He pulled her up and began shaking her. She held up her hands in front of her face to prevent him from striking her again, and Mathew shouted, "Hey, mister, you leave her alone."

"Yeah!" Mathilda cried.

The man let go of the sobbing woman and turned to face them. He was a tall, thin man with messy, dark curly hair and a strange look in his eyes. "Who are you?" he cried. "What do you want?"

"Just leave her alone," Mathew said, backing away. "Or I'll call the . . . the police."

The man turned and ran off into the bushes. The woman sank down to the ground, against the back of the boathouse, the tears pouring down her face.

"It's all right," Mathilda said softly, moving towards her. "He's gone. He's not going to hurt you anymore."

"He's a good man," the woman sobbed. "It's the drugs. They make him crazy. He doesn't mean any harm."

Mathilda reached down carefully and touched the heaving shoulder. "Don't cry," she said. "Come on, get up. You'll feel better if you . . . if you wash your face. The rest room isn't open yet. We can't go in there, but let's go over to the drinking fountain. You can get a nice drink of water and wash your face. Come on, now. Come on."

Mathilda helped her up and, speaking soothingly, led her over to the drinking fountain. The woman splashed water on her face, pulled a small dirty scarf from one pocket and began dabbing her bloody lip.

She had a nice face, Mathilda thought, a pretty face— or she would have had if her mouth wasn't bloody and there hadn't been bruise marks on her cheeks and fore-head.

"It's just in the last year," the woman said, straight-ening up and shaking her head. "He lost his job, and I got sick. Then we didn't have any money, and one of his old so-called friends gave him some crack." She held out her hands helplessly. "And now we're here, and I don't know what's going to happen to us."

Her voice choked, and Mathilda patted her arm and said gently, "Have another drink of water. Soon the stand will be open, and you can get a hot dog or maybe some coffee."

"I don't have any money," the woman wailed. "He doesn't believe me, but I really don't."

"We'll buy you something to eat. My br— I mean, my friend, Charlie, just has to make a phone call first, but you and I can go around to the other side and sit on the bench and watch the nice old lady feeding the ducks."

"What's your name, anyway?" the woman asked, al-lowing herself to be led around the side of the build-ing.

"I'm Billy, and my . . . friend there is Charlie. What's your name?"

Her name was Joanne and her boyfriend's name was Eric. She couldn't stop talking once she sat down on the bench, and even after Mathew returned, shaking his head at Mathilda, she went on and on. Only when the refreshment stand opened and Mathilda handed her a cup of coffee and a hot dog did she stop to greedily gobble down the food.

They left her there, eating, as they took their own hot dogs and Cokes and went off to another part of the lake.

"Not home," Mathew said. "The same old message on the answering machine. His name is Ben, and he's not home, and we should leave a message at the sound of the beep. Boy, this sure tastes good. Can we buy another one?"

Mathilda finished her hot dog and took a last swig of her Coke. "No," she said. "Our money's running out."

Mathew shrugged his shoulders.

"And Mathew, we forgot something."

"What?" Mathew stood up and hurried over to a bunch of logs that were piled up on the ground not far from where they sat. "Hey, Mathilda, just look at these logs. I bet we could make a raft. If I only had some rope." Mathew looked around him as if there must be a place he could find some.

"We're forgetting all about Mom and Dad," Mathilda said sharply. "We should go find a newspaper and see if they ever got our postcard."

"Oh, that's right." Mathew made a face. "Well, let's go see. And then when we get back, let's carry some of these logs over to the pavilion."

They had to go out of the park. They went by the familiar route past Uncle Ben's house where, this time, Mathilda rang his bell while Mathew watched from across the street. Nobody answered. She looked into his mailbox too, but there was nothing there. Somebody was picking up his mail. Who was it? There was something wrong, and Mathilda looked around her nervously, but the custodian, if that's who she was, did not appear.

She crossed the street again and moved Mathew along until they came to a newsstand and saw the headlines "Twins Send Card" and "Twins Run Away."

"Let's buy a newspaper," Mathilda said recklessly.

"If you want," Mathew said, "but I think we should get back to those logs before anybody else finds them."

Mathilda put twenty-five cents into the machine and drew out a newspaper. "Look, Mathew," she said, "they're still using your picture from last year."

"Who cares," Mathew said. "Can we go back now?"

"Wait! Wait! Let me just read this. Oh, I didn't know that."

"What?" Mathew fidgeted.

"That I'm bright and you're gifted."

"Oh!" Mathew was just not interested.

"Hey, listen to what Jennifer said. They even quote Jennifer."

Mathew waved a hand impatiently. "Come on, Mathilda, let's go."

"Listen, Mathew. She says, 'Mathilda is my best friend, and so is Mathew.'"

Suddenly Mathew was interested. He grabbed the newspaper and read the article. "I'm not her best friend," he shouted. "She's a liar. I'm going to call the paper and tell them."

"Oh, look there, Mathew." Mathilda pointed over his shoulder to another part of the article. "Look! It says Mom and Dad are offering a five-thousand-dollar reward to anybody who finds us, and—oh, Mathew—it says Mom and Dad say if we come home they'll let us stay together."

"I'm not her best friend," Mathew shouted.

"Mathew, did you hear what I just said? Mom and Dad say if we go home we can stay together. What do you think?"

"No," Mathew said, thinking of Jennifer. "I don't want to go home."

"But, Mathew, suppose Uncle Ben never comes home. How long can we wait?"

"Let's go get those logs," Mathew said.

# HEAT WAVE GRIPS CITY

Temperatures broke all records yesterday when the heat rose to 101 degrees. The heat is expected to continue through Thursday or Friday.

## Body Identified–
## Former Mental Patient
### Suspect Disappears

A homeless mother of 3 or 4 children, living in Golden Gate Park, has disappeared and is being sought by police. Witnesses say she attacked the murdered man after he threatened one of her children.

# TEENAGERS ARRESTED

Three teenagers were arrested yesterday for beating up two homeless men. Witnesses claim there was no provocation.

## Twins Sighted

At least 300 people have claimed that they saw Mathew Green in places as far apart as Mexico City and Toronto. The twins were also sighted in Los Angeles, Sacramento, Boise, Salt Lake City and San Francisco. Police say they are hampered in their search since so many eleven-year-old boys wear headgear.

# Ten

MATHEW BEGAN picking up items people left in the park. On Tuesday, he found a child's jump rope and a man's gray sweater. On Wednesday, he found a pocketknife, a picnic blanket, a ballpoint pen and some more rope. He kept all of his treasures hidden during the day in the bushes surrounding their pavilion.

"It's crazy the kinds of things people throw out," Mathew said early Thursday morning as he began foraging around the picnic grounds near the lake. He held up a pair of sunglasses somebody had left on a bench. "Look at this—a perfectly good pair of sunglasses." He put them on, but they were too big and slipped down his nose.

"We're running out of money," Mathilda said. "I've only got one dollar and seven cents, and you probably don't have much more. Mathew, what are you doing?"

Mathew was leaning over a garbage can near a picnic

table and pulling items out. "Just look, Mathilda, there's a bunch of fig bars left in this package from Safeway, and here's a whole chicken leg, and—wait—hey—here's a couple of chicken wings."

"Mathew!" Mathilda screamed, "get away from that garbage can. Stop it! You're getting like the rest of them."

"Mmm, this is good!" Mathew crammed a whole fig bar into his mouth and held the package towards Mathilda.

She shook her head angrily, but before she could say anything, something moved behind them. Mathilda whirled around and saw a man watching them from behind the statue of Pioneer Mother.

"Mathew," she cried, "there's somebody there. Somebody's watching us."

Someone came out slowly and moved in a strange, crooked way towards them. They recognized him instantly—the man who had been beating up the woman the other day. He looked even dirtier than he had then. There was a deep scratch on his forehead, and his hair was messy and full of pieces of paper and leaves. "Just a little change," he mumbled as he came closer. "Just a little—"

The twins ran. Across the picnic grounds, around the log cabin and up the path to the boathouse. At first they could hear the panting breath of the man pursuing them, but as they broke out into the openness of the lake, he seemed to disappear. When they looked behind them, he was nowhere to be seen.

The lake sparkled in the early morning sunshine. All was safe and comforting. The old woman, Maud, was scattering pieces of cake and bread to her assortment of friendly ducks and geese, and the little boy who seemed to shadow her was there again, a piece of angel cake in his hand, chasing after a large white goose who loudly protested his advances.

It was a sunny, warm day, and as the twins gasped, catching their breath, they could forget the menacing man in the sight of the gentle old lady feeding the colorful birds and the child playing happily around her.

"Oh, boys, boys!" the old lady called.

Mathilda looked around her. There was nobody else out yet.

"Do you mean us?" she asked.

"Yes, you two," she said with a smile. "Please come over here."

They returned her smile and hurried over to where she stood.

"I'm worried," she said, pointing to the little boy, who nearly tumbled into the lake as he tried to put his arms around an escaping mallard. "I don't know where his mother is."

The twins looked around, but except for a scarlet-suited jogger who suddenly appeared, the lake was deserted.

"I have to go now," the old woman said reluctantly, "but I am worried about leaving him by himself. I can't understand how his mother can let him run around unsupervised like she does. It's not natural. Just look." Her face turned up in a smile, and the twins followed the direction of her hand towards a family of mallards—a proud mother with six little fluffy babies swimming along together. "She doesn't let them get out of her sight for an instant. But his mother . . . she doesn't seem to care what can happen to him."

"We haven't seen her," Mathilda said. "Ever since that terrible man . . . well, we haven't seen her."

The old woman opened her purse and drew out a dollar bill. "Here," she said, handing it to Mathew. "I want you to see if you can find his mother."

She turned to look at the child who had snatched a piece of bread away from a black and white duck. Then she reached back into her purse and handed Mathew a five-dollar bill. "Get him something to eat and take him away from here or he's going to hurt himself. Find his mother and tell her to take care of him properly."

"We don't know where to look," Mathilda said.

The old woman dusted some crumbs off her neat dark blue dress and said softly, "If you need more money . . ."

"Oh, no!" Mathew said. "It's not that. We're new here. We don't really know our way around."

"New?" repeated the old woman, looking at them intently.

Mathilda stepped on his foot and said, "What my friend means is that we usually play over in the playground, and we've just started hanging around here, so we don't know this part of the park as well."

"Do your mothers know you're here?" the old woman asked crisply.

"Oh, sure!" Both twins tried to smile reassuringly, but for a moment the old lady continued looking at them searchingly.

Then she smiled, nodded and said, "As long as they

do. It's not safe, especially here, for children to be on their own." Her eyes followed the little boy, who now had his arms around a large, scolding gray-and-white goose. "Just find his mother. Then come back here tomorrow morning and tell me where she is. I think I'd better have a word or two with her myself."

"Well, we'll try, Mrs.—Mrs. . . . ."

"Everybody calls me Maud," the old woman said and turned to go.

The little boy let go of the goose, began crying as he saw her moving away and hurried over to wrap his arms around her legs.

The old woman hesitated and rested a hand on his head. "My poor boy," she murmured. "Maud has to go, but these nice boys will take good care of you. Now stop crying and you just go with them. They'll take you to your mother. Maybe if you're a good boy, they'll even buy you something nice to eat. That's right. You go along now and stay away from the lake. You'll get hurt if you don't. Go with the boys now. That's right. Good-bye."

The little boy said his name was Danny, and he held up four fingers when they asked him how old he was. They bought him a hot dog, some potato chips and a Coke. But he was still hungry when he finished, so they also bought him a bag of popcorn. He didn't offer them any at first but just filled up his fists with the popcorn and jammed it into his mouth. Pieces cascaded down the front of his dirty red sweatshirt.

"I'm hungry," Mathew said, watching him.

Danny shook his head, clutched the bag of popcorn closer to himself and looked at them out of frightened eyes.

"Don't worry, Danny," Mathilda said, "we're not going to take your popcorn. We have enough money. We can buy some for us too."

The little boy stopped eating. "Let's see the money," he said. It was the longest sentence he had spoken so far.

Mathilda held out a dime and two nickels.

"Can I have them?" Danny asked.

"No," Mathew said, "but if you tell us where your mother is, we'll give you this."

He held up a penny.

Danny shook his head and slowly picked out a piece of popcorn and put it into his mouth.

"How about this?" Mathew showed him two pennies.

"No," Danny said, but he stopped chewing and waited.

"Okay." Mathew held out a nickel. "I'll give you this, but that's my final offer."

Danny ate some more popcorn, and suddenly he held the bag out to Mathilda. "You want some?" he offered.

"Thank you," Mathilda said politely, and took a few pieces.

Solemnly Danny watched her eating. Then he turned to Mathew. "You want some?"

"Thank you." Mathew took a handful and put each piece slowly into his mouth. How wonderful it tasted! How wonderful everything tasted.

"Gimme the money!" Danny said. The twins looked at each other and smiled. Danny's voice was hoarse and deep. He almost sounded like a grown-up.

"First take us to your mother, and then we'll give you the money," Mathew told him.

Danny jumped up suddenly and began running towards a group of pigeons that had congregated along the path. He scattered the rest of the popcorn on the ground, but the frightened birds went flying out of his way.

"Crazy kid," Mathew muttered, "wasting all that popcorn on some dumb birds."

"Let's follow him," Mathilda whispered. "But don't ask him about his mother anymore. Let's just trail along behind him."

Danny stood alone inside the ring of scattered popcorn looking up at the circling birds. "Come back here!" he shouted in his deep, harsh voice. "I said come back."

Finally, he threw the empty bag down on the ground and began hurrying along the path. The twins followed behind as inconspicuously as they could. There was a mother with two children coming in the other direction. One of the children was a sleeping baby in a shiny clean stroller. The other, a little boy about Danny's age, wearing a bright blue shirt and matching shorts, was pulling a small yellow wagon with two stuffed dogs inside. Danny slowed down and stopped as he and the other boy came face to face. The other boy stopped too, and both children examined each other without speaking. Then Danny's eyes turned to the bright yellow wagon with the two stuffed dogs inside. One of the dogs was white with black floppy ears. He looked like Snoopy. The other was long and brown, like a sausage.

"Snoopy," Danny said and put out his hand to touch the black-and-white dog, but before his fingers could make any contact, the mother sprang into action. Grabbing her son firmly by the hand, she said in a loud voice, "Hurry up, Jeffrey, or we'll be late." All of them plus the wagon with the two stuffed dogs went flying down the path.

Danny turned to watch them go. He stood there silently, and suddenly Mathilda knew she had to do something. She wanted to throw a rock at the fleeing group, but that would not have changed anything for the small, dirty little boy who stood alone in the middle of the path.

Today she was wearing it, so she hurried over to where he stood. "Hey, Danny," she said, "look what I've got for you." She was already pulling it off when she reached him. "Here, it's for you. It's a Mickey Mouse watch. See, there's Mickey right in the middle, and see, he's looking right at you. Hold out your arm. I'm going to put it on your wrist."

"And I'm going to give you that nickel I showed you," Mathew shouted. "Maybe I'll give you two nickels. Maybe I'll even give you a dime."

The two of them fussed over Danny and chattered away at him. Suddenly he was no longer an unappealing, dirty, hungry pain-in-the-neck kid. Suddenly he was theirs. He belonged to them, and nobody was going to make him feel bad, if they could help it.

The startled child allowed Mathilda to strap the Mickey Mouse watch onto his wrist. He allowed Mathew to put the two nickels and the dime into his hand.

"That's Mickey," he said, looking down at the watch. Then he heaved a big sigh and smiled. "Mickey," he repeated. "That's Mickey."

He took Mathilda's hand and looked up into her face. "What's your name?"

"Billy," she told him, squeezing his hand. "And this is Charlie."

Danny didn't give his other hand to Mathew because he was looking again at the watch. Then he began pulling Mathilda along. "Let's go show Kevin," he said.

"Okay." She motioned with her head for Mathew to follow. "Let's show Kevin."

They moved down the path, past other daylight people and other children in clean clothes with bright new toys. But Danny didn't stop. He lead them over the Roman Bridge, right to the base of the waterfall. There he stopped and let go of Mathilda's hand. "Kevin," he shouted. "Kevin."

The twins looked around, but Kevin wasn't in sight. Then Danny began climbing the stairs that ran along the side of the waterfall. "Kevin," he kept shouting. "Kevin."

The day was going to be another hot one, and the twins could already feel the heat of the sun on their heads as they climbed the stairs behind Danny. Some of the cool spray from the waterfall touched their warm faces as they raced up the steps after Danny.

He never stopped. By the time they reached the top, he was already hanging over the top ledge, looking down at something in the water.

"Money!" he shouted. "Money! Lots of money!"

There were coins just under the top ledge, thrown by some of the daylight people—pennies mostly, but some nickels, dimes and even quarters—lying there on a narrow platform of rock.

Just as they reached him, he leaned over the top of the ledge and for an agonizing moment seemed to be suspended there before he disappeared. Suddenly a woman was screaming, and as the twins reached the ledge and looked over, they saw Danny hurtling downwards, silently, horribly silently, downwards inside the waterfall.

"Mathew, do something!" Mathilda shouted.

Mathew, motionless, watching in horror, saw Danny suddenly stop, wedged between two large rocks about twenty feet below them.

"We need a rope, a stick," Mathilda yelled. "We don't have anything."

A stick. A stick. Mathew remembered all the new trees that had recently been planted on both sides of the waterfall. He flew over to a young tree, supported between two poles, and forgetting that he could not possibly be strong enough to pull one of them out of the ground, pulled it out of the ground.

"Get on the other side of the waterfall, Mathilda," he shouted. She knew immediately what he meant, and she raced down the stairs on the other side. Somebody was already there, waiting for her—the battered woman named Joanne who was screeching something to Danny about holding on.

Mathew ran with the pole to the other side of the waterfall and pushed it across to where Mathilda and Joanne stood. Somebody—a man—two men, he couldn't look, were running up the stairs towards him.

"Help me! Help me!" he cried, watching as the waters seemed to be washing over Danny's face.

Mathew and the men suspended the pole across the stream and suddenly they could hear Danny's mother screaming out from above, "Danny, Danny, baby, take the pole. Put your head up. Reach for the pole! Danny!"

The little figure stirred and raised his head.

Now all of them were shouting at him.

"Take the pole!"

"Danny, reach up!"

"Hold on!"

"Danny!"

It was hanging now just above him as the mother joined Mathilda and Joanne and helped them hold the pole steady.

Slowly, obediently, the little boy reached up and hung on to the pole with both of his hands.

"Bring him this way! This way!" the mother cried.

And slowly, painfully, the little boy was lifted above the rocks and moved along shakily towards his mother.

She seemed to have the strength of twenty people as she reached out for him, snatched him out of the falls and held him fiercely against her.

"Look, Mommy," he said, holding out a bruised and bleeding arm. "Look at Mickey."

# Eleven

"He broke your watch," the man said. "That dumb kid, he went and broke your Mickey Mouse watch."

It was the man with the scarf, the one who had first admired the watch last Friday in the shelter across the street from Uncle Ben's house.

He looked up into Mathilda's face and then, puzzled, said, "But you look different. You look . . ."

Fortunately, nobody heard him. The rest of the group was intent on Danny, held tightly in his mother's arms.

"Feel his legs," said the other man, reaching over and trying to touch Danny. The little boy began crying suddenly and clung to his mother, his face buried in her chest.

"You have to make sure nothing's broken," the man continued. "I fell down a hole once over in Vietnam and broke both my legs."

It was the other man they had seen in the shelter, the

one who smelled bad and coughed, the one named Al.

"He's shivering," Joanne said. She began unwrapping a sweater from around her waist. "You'd better get those wet clothes off of him."

The little group moved up the stairs with Danny and his mother and stood around her as she tried to lay him down. He refused to let go of her, sobbing and keeping his head buried in her chest. At first, she spoke gently to him, lovingly. "My poor baby! Let Mommy see if you're all right. Just let go, Danny. Let go." Gradually, anger crept into her voice. "Let go of me— you—you—bad boy. Didn't I tell you to stay with Kevin? Didn't I tell you not to go wandering off? Didn't I?"

She began shaking him, and then everybody was talking at once. "Don't do that, lady," said the man named Al.

"Come on now, Danny," Mathilda said, "just let your mother see if you're okay."

"You should take better care of him," said Joanne.

Finally, Danny was deposited on the ground, and the man named Al began feeling his arms and legs gently, carefully.

Danny stopped crying and put his wrist up to his ear. "It's still going," he said to Mathilda.

"Nothing's broken," Al said. "Let's get him out of his wet clothes. Do you have anything else for him to wear?"

His mother pulled off his clothes. There were cuts and bruises all over Danny's body. She accepted the sweater Joanne offered her and wrapped him up in it.

"How come you let him go off like that?" Joanne

asked. "He's only a little kid. Can't you take better care of him?"

The mother's face tightened. "They're looking for me," she said. "I've got to hide until they find the killer."

"What killer?" the twins both asked at the same time.

"Where have you two been?" said the man with the scarf on his head. "Don't you know there's a killer loose here in the park?"

"Don't you read the papers?" asked the mother. "There's some crazy lunatic murdering the rest of us, and the cops are looking for . . . looking for . . ." There was a click in her throat, and her eyes blinked a few times. "They're looking for me."

Just then, her other son, Kevin, appeared, carrying the baby. The baby was crying—a weak, little cry—and the mother reached out for her and began nursing her.

"They're looking for me," she said angrily. "Me! There's a killer out there, and they think it's me."

"You?" Joanne shook her head. "Why do they think it was you?"

"Because somebody saw me scratch his face. He tried to hurt my Danny. I scratched his face, but I didn't kill him. Maybe I'm not sorry somebody else did. He made life miserable for all of us. They said he was crazy, but he was still a miserable human being."

The baby started crying again, and the mother shifted her over to her other breast.

"I don't know, lady. . . . What's your name, anyway?" asked the man with the scarf.

"Rose," said the mother, brushing a few strands of scraggly hair off the baby's face.

"Anyway, Rose," he continued, "that baby doesn't look so good. Maybe you should take her over to the hospital."

"Oh, sure," Rose said. "And then they'll take her away. They'll take them all away. You think I want to live like this? You think I like seeing my kids eating out of garbage cans?"

"Maud is looking for you," Mathew said. "She asked us to find you and tell her where you are. She gave us money to buy food for Danny. Maybe she'll help you."

"She's a cop," Rose said. "I knew it the minute I set eyes on her. She can't fool me."

"Maud." Danny sat up. His teeth were chattering, and he had a deep gash on his chin. "Maud let me feed the ducks, and she gave me some angel cake. I love Maud."

Rose made a movement towards him as if she was going to hit him. "You shut up! And keep away from her! You hear me?"

"I guess he remembers how she protected him from . . . from . . ." Mathilda began.

"How do you know about that?" Rose's eyes were fierce.

"Because I was there—my friend and I—we both were there. We saw how she protected him that time. And today she gave us money to buy him food. No wonder he likes her so much."

"She wants to take him away from me. I know what she's up to. I also know she's a cop. She wants to find me, and then they'll pin all those murders on me, and they'll take away my kids, and she'll keep Danny. . . ."

"Aw, Rose, nobody thinks it's you," said Al. "Everybody hated him. It could have been any one of us."

"But what about that poor boy?" Joanne whispered. "Or that old lady? And wasn't there somebody else too? I'm scared." Her voice began shaking. "None of us is safe."

Mathilda could feel a cold chill run down her spine, even though it was hot up there on top of Strawberry Hill. She looked over at her brother, but he was leaning forward eagerly towards Joanne. "How did they die?" he asked.

"I dunno," she said.

"Poison," Rose answered, "all three died of poison."

"A kind of poison," Al added, "that worked fast."

"How about that other body?" Joanne asked.

"What other body?"

"You know, the one near the children's playground."

"Oh, him!" Al said. "That wasn't murder. That was just a poor, old guy who was sick—like most of us—poor and sick."

The baby was sleeping now. Rose stood up and said, "I'm going to go get some dry clothes for Danny. I'll be right back." She looked down at him and said angrily, "And you'd better be here when I get back or . . ."

"That's okay, Rose," Mathilda said. "I'll take care of him until you get back." She reached out and the little boy moved painfully into her arms.

The others watched Rose disappear into the bushes, and then Joanne leaned forward and said, "There's a reward for her."

"How much?" asked the man with the scarf.

"I dunno. I saw it in the papers though." Joanne stood up and looked in the direction Rose had gone.

"Oh, don't do it," Al said. "You know it's not her.

She's like the rest of us—just down on her luck. Don't be like that. She's not the one."

"How do you know?" Joanne's eyes were still focusing off in the distance.

"I just know."

The man with the scarf was looking at Mathilda again. "You look different," he said. "What's your name?"

"Billy," she answered. "And this is my friend, Charlie. What's your name?"

"Robert," he said, looking intently at her. "But you weren't Billy then. You were different then. I remember. I remember you were different, but I don't remember how." He looked over at his friend. "Al? Do you remember, Al?" But Al started coughing, and Rose came back with some dry clothing for Danny, and Robert forgot what he was supposed to remember.

The others watched as she pulled a dirty brown shirt over Danny's head and shoved his feet through a pair of stained white shorts.

"Doesn't he have any underwear?" Mathilda asked.

Rose shook her head angrily and didn't bother to answer. She laid the baby down and began undressing her. The baby's skin was covered with purple rashes.

"Where you staying?" Joanne asked in a friendly voice. "You staying up here now?"

"None of your business where I'm staying," Rose answered. "Why do you want to know anyway?"

"Oh . . . I just . . ." Joanne examined a thread that was dangling from the hem of her skirt and began pulling on it.

"And where's that creepy friend of yours anyway?

Last time I saw him he was smacking your face. He should be locked up."

"You leave him alone." Joanne jumped up and clenched her fists. "He's . . . he's . . ."

"Okay, okay, ladies," Al said. "We got better things to do than fight. You know I been thinking, and it just came to me who it might be."

"Who what might be?" Joanne asked.

"Who the killer might be. You know, it's funny I never thought of him before, but it could be Marbles."

"Marbles? You gotta be crazy," Robert said. "Marbles can't even remember what his real name is."

Al put out a hand to stop him. "That's right. He can't remember what his name is, but he can remember all the plants you can eat, right?"

"Maybe so," Joanne said vaguely, unclenching her fists but still looking angrily over at Rose.

"And some of those plants are poisonous, right? He knows which of those are poisonous. And he's always picking up mushrooms. He knows all about mushrooms too. He spends all his time in the arboretum except when the cops pick him up for eating the plants."

"Oh, he wouldn't hurt anybody," Rose said. "Once when the baby was sick he even brewed up something for her, and the next day she was better. I've got to go find him and ask him what to do about her rashes. He'll know, and he'll help me. He's a nice man, a good man, not like . . . some of the rest." Now she looked over towards Joanne. "That friend of yours," she said, "he'd do anything for money."

"Maybe so," Al said, "but the people who were murdered didn't have any money, so it has to be somebody who has another reason."

Mathilda was listening and not listening. She was watching Mathew, and suddenly she knew she was ready to go home. She didn't want to be sitting up here on the top of Strawberry Hill with a bunch of homeless people, worrying about a crazy murderer who was loose in the park. Suddenly she was scared and cold, even though it was so hot. She wanted to go home. She had a home. She could go home. She had a mother and a father, and she missed them both so much; suddenly she couldn't believe that she and Mathew had actually run away. And she was hungry, almost hungry enough to . . . but no! Mathew had already begun eating food he found in trash cans, but she never would. Never! Never! Never!

She jumped up. "Ma—" she began, and then checked herself. "Charlie," she said. "Come on, Charlie, let's go."

He seemed totally absorbed in the conversation, and she had to lean over and shake his arm before he actually focused on her.

"We have to go," she said. "Right now! This minute! Now!"

Reluctantly he stood up and followed her.

She waited until they were halfway down the steps on the side of the waterfall before she turned to him. "I want to go home," she said. "Right now. I'm going to call home as soon as I get to the phone. I don't want to wait any longer for Uncle Ben. He's gone away, and I don't want to stay here anymore. Let's go."

"No!" Mathew said. "No!"

"Why not, Mathew?" She was crying now. "People

are being murdered in the park. I didn't know that when we ran away. I never would have come here if I'd known it. I'm scared and I'm hungry and I don't want to end up eating out of garbage cans the way you do."

She was really sobbing now, and a woman and a man who were coming up the stairs hesitated, then averted their eyes and hurried on. "We look like the rest of them now," Mathilda cried, "and I'm not going to stay here another night. I want to go home."

"I want to find Marbles," Mathew said. "Let's go look for him. He usually hangs out in the arboretum. Come on, Mathilda, let's go find him."

Mathilda stamped her foot. "I want to go home," she said. "I want to sleep in my own bed and eat food on plates. I want to be me, Mathilda Green. I like being Mathilda Green. I don't even mind my name any-more."

Mathew took a deep breath. "No!" he said. "I want to stay. I want to go find Marbles."

Mathilda said, still crying, "You don't want to stay here without me, do you, Mathew? We ran away so we could stay together. You wouldn't stay here without me, would you?"

"Of course not. But . . . listen, Mathilda. Let's stay one more night. We'll try once more to call Uncle Ben, but if he doesn't come by tomorrow, we'll call Mom and Dad. Just one more night, okay?"

"I'm scared," Mathilda said. "I want to go home. Right now."

"Just one more night," Mathew insisted. "One more night."

"But why?" Mathilda sobbed. "Why do we have to wait another night?"

"Because I want to find Marbles."

"Why?"

"There's a reason why." Mathew's face was glowing, like it usually did when he was working on some complicated model. "There's something in my mind . . . something I need to figure out about those murders, something that I nearly understand. . . ."

Mathilda was still crying. "What is it?"

Mathew shook his head. "I don't know yet, but I want to go find Marbles."

"Suppose he's the murderer?" Mathilda was crying so hard now, she could hardly talk. "Why would you want to find a murderer?"

Through the corner of her eye, she could see Joanne hurrying down the steps on the other side of the waterfall. She's going to call the police and tell them about Rose and Danny and the other kids, Mathilda thought. Mathew was saying something to her, but she couldn't hear what it was because there was an anger in her so great, it was even bigger than her fear. Nobody was going to hurt Danny. Nobody. Not if she could help it.

"Joanne!" she shouted. "Joanne, stop!"

Joanne did not even turn to see who was calling her name. She hurried even faster down the stairs.

Mathilda turned and ran up the stairs.

"Where are you going?" Mathew shouted.

"We've got to warn Rose," Mathilda said. "Joanne's going to turn her in. Hurry! Hurry!"

# Police Baffled by Park Murders

## *SUSPECTS QUESTIONED*

Three homeless men and two women were questioned by police in connection with the three park murders. The mystery woman who had attacked the last victim has still eluded police. A reward has been offered for information leading to her discovery.

### *Neighborhood Groups Demand Homeless Be Driven From Park*

## TWINS SIGHTED IN DENVER

Mathew and Mathilda Green are now believed to be hiding somewhere in Denver. Reliable witnesses claim to have seen them both last Friday in the Denver Greyhound Bus Depot. The distraught parents beg the children to contact them and will agree to any conditions they set.

# San Francisco Giants Blank L.A. Dodgers 10 to 0

Heat wave should end tonight. Fog expected to return.

# Twelve

Rose said, "Anybody who thinks Marbles is a killer has got to be crazy. Just look at him. That's all you have to do. Just look."

Mathew and Mathilda looked. They saw a short, thin old man with clothes that fit him too loosely and shoes that swam on his feet. They watched him lean over a plant in the Garden of Fragrance, examine it, pick it carefully, hold it under his nose, take what looked like a salt shaker out of his pocket, salt it, nibble at a piece of it, stop, consider, sprinkle a little more salt and swallow the rest of it.

The twins began laughing, but then a man who looked like a gardener, holding a pair of pruning shears in one hand, hurried up to Marbles and began arguing with him.

The twins moved closer and heard the gardener say, ". . . absolutely the last time, Marbles. You have to stop it."

"Good morning," Marbles said, smiling pleasantly. "I don't think the lemon geranium is doing as well as last year. Possibly too much acid in the soil but . . ."

"Why don't you go and eat some nasturtiums," the gardener said. "I don't mind if you eat the nasturtiums or the miner's lettuce or even the wild strawberries, but you have to leave the lemon geranium alone. You keep eating it, and there's hardly anything left."

". . . but the chamomile is doing very nicely, and so is the sage."

"Marbles, are you listening?" the gardener said. "I don't want to have to call the police again."

"Police?" said Marbles. "They don't know anything about plants. I'd be happy to give them my orientation lecture, but I am rather pressed this morning, so good day to you, and watch that acid soil."

He smiled kindly at the gardener, reached over and patted a plant as if it were an old friend and came slowly down the path to where Rose and the children stood.

"Good morning, Marbles," Rose said.

"Good morning to you," he said courteously and put up his hand as if to tip a hat that was not on his head. He was an old man, a very old man, with a wrinkled skin that fit his face as loosely as his clothes fit his body.

"The baby isn't coughing anymore," Rose said, "thanks to you. But her rash is much worse."

Marbles looked over his shoulder at the gardener, who still stood in the Garden of Fragrance watching him. "A few young leaves of chicory ground into a paste might do the trick," he whispered, "but perhaps

we had better go elsewhere this morning. I also wanted
to check on the thimbleberry bushes, and I did notice a
bunch of nice, tender tule shoots yesterday, or maybe it
was the day before yesterday. . . ."

He was talking to himself as he began walking away
and hardly seemed to notice that Rose, her children
and the twins were tagging right along behind him.
Every so often, he would stop, pick a leaf or a blossom
from a plant, put a little salt on it and eat it. He was
quite willing to share his expertise with the others, and
Mathew and Mathilda found themselves tasting an assortment of leaves, flowers and young shoots.

"I like hot dogs better," Danny complained as the
old man rambled on and on about "Nature's bounty."

The twins noticed that Rose seemed oblivious to
Marbles' eccentricity, chattering away to him about her
children's skin rashes, runny noses and infected
scratches. Whenever she needed an answer, she would
put a hand on his arm and say, "Marbles, are you listening to me?"

"Of course I am, my dear. You were saying skin
rashes, and we were going to find you some chicory,
weren't we?"

"I've also got to hide somewhere," she said. "The
police are looking for me. I know you're staying behind
that little nursery in the arboretum, and I wondered if
you'd mind if we stayed there with you just for a day or
two. Until the baby is better. Then, I guess I'll have to
move on."

There was that click in her voice again, and Mathilda
said, "Isn't there someplace you could go? Don't you
have a family?"

"No," Rose said. "No family. No place to go."

Marbles was clapping his hands together over a clump of large, prickly plants with one yellow flower that rose up high in its midst. "The century plant is in bloom," he said rapturously. "I have had my eye on this one for a long, long time."

"Century plant?" Mathew asked. "Does it really bloom only once every century?"

"No." Marbles smiled indulgently. "Not really every century. Maybe every thirty years or so. After it blooms, the whole plant dies, and a new young one grows up out of the old. The Indians used the young stalks as a staple food, and the juice from the roots was used for wounds and scratches." Marbles cleared his throat, straightened up and continued lecturing. He pointed with his hands as if there were a blackboard behind him and a roomful of students in front of him.

Rose said proudly, "He used to be a professor somewhere. Weren't you, Marbles? Weren't you a professor somewhere?"

But Marbles was deep into his lecture now and didn't hear her.

"Caruso, too," Rose said. "He was a great singer once. He sang all over the world." Rose's face creased up. "I haven't seen him for days now. I mean, I haven't heard him."

"Oh, we did," Mathilda said. "He woke us up last . . . last . . . When was it, Charlie?"

Mathew didn't answer. He wasn't listening to her. He was listening to Marbles, and then, slowly, he moved closer to him and watched as Marbles reached up, pulled a small blossom off the century plant, salted it and put it into his mouth.

"Funny, how you forget about time," Mathilda said to Rose. "We saw Caruso. . . . He woke us up one morning. It was a few days ago, but I don't remember exactly which day it was."

"They all get to be the same," Rose said wearily. She sat down suddenly on the ground, laid the baby in her lap and began rocking her. "I haven't heard Caruso for a while, and now I'm worried about him. He's a pest when he's around because he sings when everybody's sleeping. And yet when he's not around, it's kind of strange. It's kind of too quiet."

"Rose," Mathilda said, "how did this happen to you? Didn't you ever have a home?"

"Sure I had a home," Rose said, "like anybody else. But my husband took off, and I couldn't pay the rent. Now I don't know where to go. The shelters are terrible places—they're worse than being outside."

Kevin was chewing on some leaves Marbles had given him and Mathew.

"How do you know, Marbles, which plants are good for you, and which ones aren't?" Mathew asked.

"Books," Marbles said. "Learning. Books and learning." Marbles' voice was reverential. "Knowledge comes through books and learning. Some of these plants can make you sick; some of these plants can kill you. . . ."

Mathilda felt sleepy. She heard Mathew's voice questioning Marbles, and Marbles' voice answering, but she wasn't really listening. The sun was warm on her head, and everything was green and good all around them.

Suddenly Rose leaped up and yelled, "Danny! Danny!"

Mathilda broke out of her doze and jumped up also, wide-awake immediately.

"I can't stop him," Rose said angrily. "If I take my eyes off him for one second, he's off. I just don't know what to do with him."

Mathilda put a soothing hand on her arm. "He's probably back at the lake. I'll go and look for him there."

"It's that Maud," Rose said. "He only wants to be with her. I hate her."

"No, no. Maud won't be there now. She only comes early in the morning."

"I hate her," Rose repeated. "She's a cop. I know she is. And she wants to take him away from me."

"I don't think she's a cop," Mathilda said, "but she does like him a lot and worry about him. Let me go and look for him. You'll be staying with Marbles behind the little nursery in the arboretum. I'll look for him and bring him back to you."

"Don't tell anybody where I am," Rose said. "Especially that Joanne. I don't trust her."

Mathew was still talking to Marbles. Mathilda called out, "Charlie! Charlie! Let's go look for Danny. He took off again. I'm going back to the lake to find him. Let's go."

"No!" Mathew said. "I'm busy now."

Mathilda hesitated. "I have to go and find him," she said. "I have to go right now."

"Just wait a few minutes." Mathew waved an impatient hand and continued his conversation with Marbles.

"I can't wait," she said, beginning to hurry off. "I'll meet you over at the nursery later on. As soon as I find Danny, I'll bring him back there."

Mathilda was right. Danny had returned to the lake. But to her great surprise, so had Maud. She found them both as she hurried over to the boathouse. Just in time too. Maud was leading Danny away. She called out, "Maud! Maud! Stop!"

Maud turned and stood there, holding Danny by the hand, watching as Mathilda raced up to them.

"I knew he'd be here," she said. "I told Rose he'd be here, but I've never seen you here so late in the morning. It must be nearly noon."

"I was worried," Maud said.

"Oh, you don't have to worry about Danny anymore," Mathilda began eagerly, but then she stopped. Yes, she thought. After tomorrow, Mathew and I will be going home, and who will worry about Danny? She looked up into Maud's soft, worried face, and she thought he would be better off with her. She would feed him properly and look after him. Maybe it would be best if she took him.

"Where is his mother?" Maud asked.

I should tell her, Mathilda thought. If she's a cop, she could take them all to a place that's at least warm and safe, and where the children could be looked after. Rose . . . well, Mathilda didn't think Rose was the killer, but if she wasn't, then maybe the police could help her find a home.

But she remained silent, and Maud said sadly, "I knew she wouldn't be able to look after him properly. I knew it. I hoped she would, but she's too far gone . . . too hopeless. . . ."

"Oh, I don't know," Mathilda said weakly. "She can't help herself. She doesn't have any money, and she's trying, but . . ."

Danny pulled at Maud's hand impatiently. "Come on, Maud, let's go." He turned to Mathilda. "Maud's going to get some more bread and cake, and then we're going to come back and feed the ducks some more. Maud's going to let me come home with her. Right, Maud?"

"I told his mother I'd bring him right back to her," Mathilda said, almost apologetically. "Come on, Danny, we'd better go right now."

"But I want to go home with Maud," Danny said. "I want to see where Maud lives."

Maud sighed, and Mathilda could see how reluctantly she dropped Danny's hand. "You go along with the boy now, dear," she said. "Another day you'll come home with me."

"I want to go now," Danny said, putting his arms around her legs.

Maud patted his head and shook her own. "It's so sad," she said. "So terribly sad that this poor child has nobody taking care of him."

"I'll take care of him, Maud. I promise," Mathilda said.

Danny cried and cried when Maud left. At first he refused to take Mathilda's hand, so she picked him up and began carrying him away.

"I hate you," he said, struggling in her arms. "I hate you and I love Maud."

"Listen, Danny," she said. "How would you like me to tell you a story?"

"No. I want to go home with Maud."

"Well, you're going to like this story. It's all about a duck. Okay, here goes: *Once upon a time, there was an ugly duckling. . . .*"

After a time, Danny stopped struggling and began listening intently to the story. Mathilda was able to set him down, hold his hand and lead him away to the arboretum. She added many details that weren't in the original story and kept it going until they reached the nursery, where Rose, Marbles and Mathew were supposed to meet her. None of them were there.

"So then what happened?" Danny asked.

"I've just told you. *The ugly duckling became a big, beautiful swan, and he lived happily ever after.*"

"Tell me another one," Danny said.

"I will, but let's see if we can find your mother first."

Danny sat down on the ground. "I'm tired," he said. "I'm hungry."

Mathilda hesitated. She knew Danny could not be trusted to stay in one place for very long. She put her hand into her pocket and felt only two dimes. Enough for a phone call. Not enough for anything to eat for Danny.

"Let's go look for your mother, Danny," she said. "Maybe she'll have something for you to eat."

"You go look," he said. "I'll stay here."

"Come on, Danny," Mathilda said. "I'll tell you another story."

"About another duck?"

"No, about a little boy. A little boy named Danny."

Danny stood up and took her hand.

*"Once upon a time,"* she began as she walked around the nursery, holding on to his hand, *"there was a boy named Danny."*

She moved out onto the green lawn where families sat together eating picnic food and playing picnic games. No Rose. No Marbles. No Mathew.

*"This boy was very kind. He loved birds and used to come to the pretty lake in the park every day and play with them."*

"Say it again," Danny said. "Say it again."

She did and retraced her steps back to the nursery. On one side was the entrance to the Redwood Nature Trail, a dense, forested path that led into a grove of redwood trees. It seemed to her that she could hear voices, but she hesitated at the entrance. "Marbles!" she called. "Rose! Uh . . . Charlie!"

"And then what happened?"

Nobody answered her, but now she was certain she could hear voices inside the grove.

*"Well, Danny's favorite duck was one called Lawrence."*

"No, no," Danny said. "I like Henry better. Maud says he's the friendliest. Say I like Henry better."

Holding tightly to Danny's hand, Mathilda led him into the redwood grove. *"So Danny's favorite duck was the one called Henry. One day when Danny was playing with Henry, Henry said to him, 'Hello, Danny.'*

*" 'I didn't know ducks could talk,' Danny said.*

*" 'Well, usually they can't,' Henry said, 'but I'm a magic duck and I can speak.' "*

Deeper and deeper into the redwood grove, Mathilda walked with Danny. There was very little sun through the high trees, and the air smelled damp and old. Somebody was speaking as they moved farther along the path. It was a man's voice. A familiar one.

Danny tugged at her hand. "What did Henry say? Say what he said."

Mathilda continued. *"So Henry said to Danny, 'I'm a magic goose, and I can grant you three wishes.' "*

"What does that mean?" Danny asked, looking up into her face.

He was so small and so thin, and his eyes were so big, Mathilda reached down and picked him up again in her arms and pulled him against her. "It means you can have something that you want. That's what a wish is. You have to say what you want and then you get it. In the story, the duck, Henry, says that Danny can have three wishes."

"I know, I know," Danny said. "I know what they are. I want to go home with Maud."

The path led into an opening where benches made of redwood trees faced towards a pulpit also made of redwood. Standing behind it was Marbles, lecturing to an imaginary class on the subject of mushrooms and other fungi.

"Marbles," Mathilda cried. "Where's Rose?"

Marbles' hand, which had been pointing to an invisible blackboard, remained suspended in the air. "Rose?" he said. "Rose?"

"Rose," Mathilda said. "You remember Rose. She's Danny's mother. She has a baby with a rash, and another little boy named Kevin. She was going to stay with you. Where is she now?"

"Oh, Rose!" Marbles nodded and put down his hand. "Yes, I remember Rose."

"Where is she?"

"She went away . . . with four policemen. I don't think she wanted to go, and I tried to show them some new passionflowers, but they showed no interest at all." Marbles shook his head, and his finger began moving upwards once more.

"But my brother—where is my brother?" Mathilda cried. "Did the police take him too?"

"Who is your brother?" Marbles asked, looking intently at her.

Mathilda heard a rustling behind her and without looking to see who it was, she ran back down the path, clutching Danny close to her and sobbing in terror.

# Thirteen

MATHEW HAD SAID, "Tell Billy to wait for me. Tell him I'll be right back."

"Yes, I will," Rose had promised.

He had helped her move her belongings behind the small nursery in the arboretum and left her there with Marbles, who was mixing up a paste of chicory and water to put on the baby's rashes.

He hurried along, reciting the names Marbles had given him over and over again, so he wouldn't forget: *Amanita virosa*—Destroying Angel; *Amanita phalloides*—death cup; *Gyromitra californica*—false morel. But on the way, he noticed a partly empty package of corn chips lying on top of one trash can, and then half of a peanut butter and jelly sandwich on top of another. By the time he reached the small bookstore at the end of the arboretum, he had forgotten all the names except Destroying Angel.

"Do you have a book on mushrooms?" he asked the man at the counter.

"Of course," said the man, remaining behind the counter.

"Well, could I see it please?"

"You'd better go and wash your hands first," said the man, inspecting him with disapproval. "Unless you plan on buying the book immediately."

"I'll wash my hands," Mathew said, looking down at his hands, all green and grimy from handling the leaves and bulbs Marbles had shown him, and with salty specks of crumbled corn chips sticking to them. He hurried into the men's room, scrubbed his hands, dashed some water on his face and returned to the store.

All of the poisonous mushrooms were there in the mushroom handbook that the man had showed him. The *Amanita virosa* was pure white and innocent-looking, the *Amanita phalloides* was pale green and not so innocent-looking and the *Gyromitra californica* was a wrinkled, evil-looking muddy brown. All of them could be dried and ground into somebody's food, but none of them acted as swiftly as the poison that had killed each of the murder victims.

People kept bumping into him and reaching over and under him as he stood there in the small store, absorbed in the book. When he had finished reading what he needed to know, he put the book back on its shelf and then stood thoughtfully for a moment or two trying to put it all together. There was something inside his mind that had been troubling him ever since he'd first heard about the murders, something that he couldn't quite locate. Finally he left the store, certain that Marbles was not the murderer.

There was a phone on one side of the building. Mathew drew out the change in his pocket and counted it. Thirty-seven cents. He was hungry. He was always hungry now, but he knew that he could usually find something to eat anytime he cared to check the trash cans.

This would be the last time, because tomorrow he had agreed to go home. Home! He thought about Mom and Dad and shook his head. No! He didn't want to go home. He didn't want to go to that home where he could only be himself inside his own room. In one week, the park had become his home, and if Mathilda would agree, he could stay longer. He could learn from Marbles how to recognize all the healthy foods growing right here in the park. He could learn, as the Indians had, how to make use of the many reeds and grasses to make a shelter for Mathilda and himself. He didn't want to go home. At least, he didn't want to go to that home.

He fingered the change in his hand and considered. Mathilda wanted to go home, and he had promised. Tomorrow, he had agreed. Unless! Unless he could figure out another way—a better way than going back to that uneasy, scary place he used to call home.

Scary? Was it more scary than living here in the park with a murderer loose among them? Strange, how he wasn't worried about the murderer. And why was that? He seemed to know, somewhere inside his head, who that murderer was and that he was safe from him.

He dialed the number. He knew it by heart now. And he knew the message too, reciting it along with the voice. "Hello. This is Ben. I'm sorry I cannot come to the phone right now, but if you'll leave a message and your phone number at the sound of the beep, I'll return your call as soon as I can."

This time, at the sound of the beep, Mathew left a message. "Uncle Ben," he said, "this is me. Mathew. Mathilda and I have been living in the park all week, waiting for you to come back. We've run away, and we want to stay with you. Please, Uncle Ben, come back today. Tomorrow will be too late. Come to the boat-house in the park. I'll be looking for you. Please come, because if you don't, we'll have to go back to our parents."

When he hung up, he remembered that Mathilda would be looking for him over at the nursery. He hurried along the path and tried not to think about tomorrow. Unless Uncle Ben got his message and came to the park, today would be his last day here.

So many things he wanted to do in the park. If they could stay with Uncle Ben, the park would still be his, would still lie there, across the street from his uncle's house. He had been collecting logs without really knowing what he wanted to do with them. Now he knew. He wanted to make a raft to float on Stow Lake—not during the day, of course, but later, when everybody had gone home. Mathilda could come too, if she wanted. He could make a raft big enough for the two of them, and they could float there past the water-fall, under the Roman Bridge, and watch the water catch all the pinks and blues of the setting sun. Maybe today he could build the raft. He had been collecting rope and cord. It wouldn't be hard to put it all together. He hadn't made anything for a couple of weeks now, and his fingers began flexing in anticipation.

Mathilda wasn't at the nursery. Neither was Rose or Marbles. The only one who was there, sitting on a bench and reading a crumpled newspaper, was Joanne.

"Did you see my—uh—friend?" he asked.

Joanne looked up from the newspaper. "Which friend?" she asked.

"My friend Billy." He didn't like the way she was looking at him, and he decided that he didn't like her. That was a new feeling for him—not liking somebody and feeling okay about it.

"Oh, him!" Joanne said. "Sure I saw him—about fifteen minutes ago. He was running like a hundred wolves were after him. Holding on to that goofy-looking kid who fell in the waterfall." Joanne began laughing. Mathew noticed that her teeth were discolored, and he took a step backwards.

"Well, why was she—I mean, he—why was he running like that?"

"I dunno." Joanne stopped laughing, and her face turned sour again. She leaned forward. "But you missed the big show. Before that. When the cops came and took her away—that was really something."

"They took her away," Mathew repeated, and suddenly there was nothing left inside of him but a big, empty hole. He could feel the tears beginning to roll down his face.

"That really was something," Joanne said grimly. "She tried to run away, but she couldn't get very far with that other goofy kid hanging on to her and the baby screeching away. And then Marbles—it would have been funny if it wasn't for Rose carrying on the way she did—but Marbles, he thought they were coming to get him, and he was chewing on one of his plants, and he started spitting it out all over the place. I tell you—you really missed something." Joanne smiled as if she were remembering some pleasant memory.

"Wait a minute," Mathew said. "Who did you say the police arrested?"

"I just told you," Joanne said. "They got Rose and her two kids. Then Marbles disappeared. And then your friend came back with that other kid and went looking for all of you. I saw it all, but I didn't tell the cops. Maybe you think I did, but I didn't."

Mathew wiped his face. "I thought you said the police arrested Billy."

"I never said that. I said they arrested Rose. She was the one. I never said anything about Billy." Joanne leaned forward. "Why would they want Billy anyway? What did he do?"

"He didn't do anything," Mathew said, trying hard not to let his feelings of dislike for her show too plainly. "But where did he go?"

"I dunno." Joanne leaned back and picked up her newspaper again.

Mathew studied her angrily. He was sure she must have told the police where Rose was. She did it for the reward, and if she knew who he and Mathilda were, she'd turn them in too. I hate her, he thought. She's a miserable woman, and if that weirdo boyfriend of hers ever beats her up again, I won't do anything to stop him.

Carefully, so that his voice wouldn't register his thoughts, he asked, "Which way did Billy go?"

"That way." Joanne pointed without raising her face from the newspaper. "He's probably looking for you. Why don't you tell me where you'll be so I can tell him if he comes back."

"Thank you," he said coldly, "but I don't know where I'll be." Then he hurried off in the direction Joanne had pointed.

He thought he knew where Mathilda would be, and he was right. Back at Stow Lake, in front of the Chinese pavilion. She was sitting near the lake, watching Danny as he tried to feed the ducks and geese with handfuls of grass. She was trying to keep an eye on Danny and be on the lookout for Mathew at the same time. When she saw him, she jumped up, and her face brightened with happiness and relief.

"Oh, Mathew, wait till you hear what happened."

No, he thought to himself. No. I wouldn't want to live here in the park or even with Uncle Ben if she wasn't here too.

". . . and I guess I just panicked there in the redwood grove, but I don't think anybody was really after me," Mathilda was saying.

"I heard about Rose," he told her. "Joanne told me."

Mathilda looked over at Danny as he began throwing sand at the water birds. "Don't do that, Danny," she said. Then she lowered her voice. "I think Joanne told the police where Rose was. I think she did it for the reward."

"I do too," Mathew said.

"I hate her." Mathilda clenched her fists. "I'm glad she doesn't know about us. I wouldn't want her to make any money because of us."

"Me neither," Mathew said.

"Listen, Mathew." Mathilda lowered her voice. "I have an idea. We're going home tomorrow, right?"

Mathew shook his head sadly. "We are if Uncle Ben doesn't come home. I left a message on his answering machine."

Mathilda waved her hand impatiently. "He won't come home. He must have gone away on a trip. That's what I think, but okay, we'll wait until tomorrow because I made up my mind about Danny."

"What about Danny?"

She was whispering now. "I'm going to let him go with Maud. He loves her, and I know she wants him. Tomorrow morning, I'll tell her what's happened, and then you and I will go home."

"If Uncle Ben doesn't come," Mathew agreed.

"He won't." Mathilda quickly moved over to Danny, who was now throwing rocks at the scattering birds.

For the rest of the afternoon, Mathew worked on his raft. He pulled a bunch of logs over to a place on the island where he could work and keep an eye on the boathouse. He forgot to be hungry, and when Mathilda and Danny brought him some soggy french fries in a McDonald's wrapper and a bag of crushed cherries, he looked up at them in surprise. "Where did you get these?" he asked.

Mathilda didn't answer, but Danny said proudly, "I showed him where to look. The best can is the one up behind the parking lot, but he didn't know."

Mathilda shrugged and said quickly, "There's no money left—and he's hungry. I'm hungry too. When you're hungry, you can't be fussy."

Late in the afternoon, Danny fell asleep, and Mathilda came to sit down next to her brother and to help him put the finishing touches on the raft.

"We can both go out on it tonight," Mathew said. "It's big enough for the two of us."

"Can we take Danny too?" Mathilda wanted to know.

"We'd better not," Mathew said. "He wouldn't sit still, and he'd fall off."

"Well, you go then. I don't have to go."

"Maybe after he's asleep, we both can go."

"It's too dark on the lake then."

"I'd like to take it out before it gets dark. After the boathouse closes and when everybody goes home, but before it gets completely dark."

"That's okay. I'll stay with Danny." She looked down at where the sleeping child lay, all curled up with a dirty hand resting against a dirty face. "I'm going to miss him," she said, "but Maud will take good care of him."

Mathew tied and knotted a piece of rope, and the raft was finished. "Look," he said, "it's all finished now, Mathilda."

"That's nice," she said vaguely. Her mind was on something else. "Mathew," she asked, "do you think Mom and Dad missed us very much?"

Mathew raised the finished raft from the ground and shook it gently. "I don't know," he said. "What do you think?"

"I think they did," she answered. "And maybe it was wrong to run away."

"They were going to separate us," Mathew said. "Don't you remember?"

"Yes," she said. "I was forgetting. But now they won't. After we come home, I know they won't try to separate us ever again."

Mathew looked over at the boathouse. He still hoped

that Uncle Ben would show up. It was a busy, crowded scene with daylight people getting into and out of boats. Children and grown-ups crowded around the refreshment stands, and dogs chased each other up and down. But in all that crowd, he could not find his uncle anywhere.

# Fourteen

THE FOG RETURNED by late afternoon. Wisps of it snaked through the tall grasses bordering the lake and hovered over the waters. Suddenly the heat wave was over. Those who had them put on sweaters and coats, and those who didn't shivered. Most of the people out on the lake in rowboats, motorboats or paddle boats, began thinking of warm dinners in warm houses and turned back towards the shore. Others, lolling in front of the boathouse or on benches around the lake, quickly packed up picnic baskets, collected children and headed for home. By six o'clock, except for a single jogger, the lake was deserted.

"I'm cold," Danny whimpered, even after Mathilda had pulled her sweater over his head. It hung down below his knees, and she had to roll the sleeves up until they formed big, heavy doughnuts above his wrists.

"I'm hungry," Danny also complained, but that was a problem much easier to solve. The heat had brought out so many picnickers, and they all had so much to eat, and had left so quickly, that the remains of their feasts overflowed trash cans and, in some cases, were simply scattered across lawns and benches.

"Here, Danny, try a piece of this chicken," Mathew urged.

"Have a little potato salad," Mathilda offered.

The food was more varied than usual—chicken, potato salad, carrot and celery sticks, loads of French bread, more half-filled cans of Coke than they could drink, cookies, cakes, half-eaten candy bars. . . . Nobody was hungry when they had finished.

"I'm cold," Danny repeated after they had eaten.

"Why don't you go fly those gliders with Danny?" Mathilda suggested to Mathew. "If he runs around, he'll get warm."

"What gliders?" Mathew asked.

"You remember. The ones you bought at the hobby store the first day we came here."

It seemed like years ago. "I remember," Mathew said, shrugging his shoulders. "But I don't remember what happened to them." All he could think of now was his raft.

Mathilda wrapped up Danny in the picnic blanket Mathew had found some days earlier, but his teeth chattered, and he kept saying he was cold.

"Let's jog, Danny," Mathilda said. "We'll jog around the lake."

"I'm cold," Danny said. "I don't want to jog."

"Maybe we can jog over to the boathouse. We can see if there's any popcorn left in the popcorn machine."

"Can we feed the ducks with it?" Danny asked. "Will Maud be there?"

"We can feed the ducks," Mathilda said, "but Maud won't be there until tomorrow."

Danny jumped up, and Mathew watched as the two of them started off down the path to the Roman Bridge. He was disappointed that the fog had returned. In his mind, he had seen himself out on the raft, drifting along on the waters of Stow Lake, all pink and blue in the setting sun. But now, with the fog hanging over the lake, veiling the sun, there would be no pinks and blues—only grays.

His own teeth were chattering as he stood up and carried the raft over to the lake. He supposed this would be his first and last chance to try out the raft. Even he had to admit that his uncle would probably not return before tomorrow. Carefully he moved the raft out onto the water. It floated. Even more carefully he eased himself on top of it. It continued to float. He pushed himself off from the island and slowly stood up. It kept right on floating.

"Mathilda," he shouted. "Mathilda! Look at me, Mathilda!"

But she was out of sight and probably couldn't hear him either.

Pride rose up in him. Pride at his raft, and pride at himself for being on it alone, there in the middle of Stow Lake. He felt like a king, surveying his domain. It was all his—and the moment, foggy and cold as it was, belonged to him.

Mathew had fashioned an oar for himself out of a broken paddle-ball racket he'd found and attached it to a long, thin branch. He began paddling. He decided to go around the island in the opposite direction Mathilda and Danny had taken and surprise them at the boathouse. She and Danny would certainly be there by the time he arrived, and he couldn't wait to see the look on her face when he came paddling along on his raft.

The lake narrowed before it reached the old stone bridge, and a single jogger, going in the opposite direction on the mainland side, raised a hand in greeting but did not pause. Mathew waved back. He could just make out the jogger's face, and he looked familiar—a tall man with dark curly hair, wearing a bright red sweat suit. Perhaps he had seen him jogging before, Mathew thought vaguely. There were quite a few joggers who regularly ran around the lake.

Mathew paddled languorously and felt the raft move gently beneath his feet. He had enjoyed putting it together. But perhaps it would not be such a terrible thing going home and having his room to himself again. His fingers tightened around the paddle. He had a number of future space projects waiting for him. There were the two beautiful ones he'd seen at the hobby store that he was certain his parents would buy for him—the Mercury Redstone and the Crusader Swing-Wing.

But no! Suddenly he realized that those space projects no longer interested him, just as the bus terminal and the service station no longer interested him. Now it seemed such a long time ago that he had planned on dismantling some of those earlier projects in order to make room for his space models. Now none of them interested him. Something else would have to take their place. But what?

Another time he would decide. Right now, all that

really mattered was being alone on the lake with the scores of ducks and geese that came and went in the fog. They were talking to each other and perhaps to him. After tomorrow, he and Mathilda would not be there, would not be waking up in the morning, safe inside their Chinese pavilion with the sound of the waterfall in their ears and the sound of the water birds talking to each other.

Safe? Yes, he had felt safe. And even now, thinking about the three park murders, he still felt safe. Gently he moved his paddle and thought about the murders. It seemed to him again that he should know who the murderer was. Not Marbles—the poison in those mushrooms worked too slowly. Caruso? No—he was sure it was not Caruso. But how could he be so sure, and why did he seem to know that it was somebody who did not threaten him?

One more turn now, and the boathouse would be in sight. He would see Mathilda and Danny, probably feeding the birds. It was so cold now, he could feel shivers down his neck and arms. Tonight they would have to pile all of their clothes and lots of leaves and branches over them to stay warm.

Now the boathouse was in sight, and yes, even through the heavy fog, he could make out Mathilda and Danny. They weren't feeding the ducks, though. They were talking to somebody. His heart began pounding. Uncle Ben? Was it Uncle Ben? No. It wasn't Uncle Ben. It was Maud, and she was holding out something to them.

Mathew watched as they both reached out their hands, and then, suddenly, at a distance, running out of the fog, and visible only because of his bright red suit, the jogger appeared, shouting and holding something in his hand. He was too far away for Mathew to see it clearly, but it was something very scary. And then, from the opposite direction, another person came running, and even with the fog veiling her, Mathew knew who it was. Joanne, her hair streaming behind her. Joanne, screaming like a maniac, and too far away for Mathilda to hear.

Only Mathew standing on his raft in Stow Lake could see them both approaching and hear them. And he knew then who the murderer was and that he was not safe and neither was Mathilda or Danny.

"Mathilda! Mathilda!" he shouted as Joanne, shrieking and waving her fists, grew closer and closer. "Watch out, Mathilda! Stop, Mathilda, stop!"

She saw and heard him before she saw and heard Joanne. She put up her hand to wave. There was something in her hand. He had to get over to her and warn her. He began paddling furiously, but he had moved over too far to one side of the raft, and it tipped over. He tried to scream out to her, but then, just as the waters closed over his head, he heard the sound of a shot.

# Fifteen

UNCLE BEN did not return from his trip to Baja for another ten days. As soon as he did and heard the news, he came out to see Mathew and Mathilda. He found them in Mathew's room, dismantling the last of the space models.

"I'm sorry," he said to them. "I'm sorry I wasn't home. My custodian told me when I got back that she had seen a couple of boys ringing my bell, but I never thought it might be you two. She was picking up my mail for me and looking after my apartment while I was gone. I'm sorry."

The twins looked at him in surprise. They couldn't remember why he should feel sorry.

"Why are you sorry?" Mathilda finally asked.

"Because you needed me, and I wasn't home when you did. I know it was a terrible time for you—for all of you—and if I had been home, none of it would have happened."

"You couldn't know," their mother said gently.

"Of course not," their father agreed.

The grown-ups all sighed in agreement, and the twins looked at each other and tried not to smile.

"But thank goodness you're both fine now," Uncle Ben continued, "and nobody was really hurt."

"Except . . ." Mathew began.

"Well, of course, except for those poor homeless people. But you guys are really heroes—I read that the police say you both helped them in preventing a fourth murder and in capturing the murderer."

Now the twins didn't feel like smiling. "It was my fault," Mathilda said. "I should have figured it out."

"No, no, it was mine," Mathew said. "I saw it—that time up on Strawberry Hill. It didn't register for a while, but it should have."

"How about some lunch?" Dad said brightly. "We could all go to Burger King."

"No!" Mathew said. "I hate hamburgers. I've always hated hamburgers."

"Well, how about a pizza? I could have one delivered."

Uncle Ben sat down on Mathew's bed. "This is a big room," he said. "I guess I haven't been here for a long time, but I don't remember that your room was so big and so . . . so empty."

"It's because he had it all piled up with his models," Mom said sadly. "He says he's not interested in models anymore."

"So what about a pizza? I could order one with pepperoni or mushrooms—whatever you like, Mathew."

"Mushrooms," Mathew said. "And pepperoni."

"And green peppers and onions and extra cheese," Mathilda added. "I'm starving."

"So am I," Mathew said. "How about getting two extra-large, Dad?"

"Sure thing, son," his father said happily. "I'll just go call in the order."

Their mother laughed out loud. "These kids are hungry all the time now," she said. "There's no way to keep up with their appetites. I think Mathew must have gained ten pounds since he came home—and Mathilda—well, Mathilda just never stops eating."

"Do you feel like talking about it?" their uncle asked. "I still don't understand what happened at the end."

"Maybe the less said about that the better," Mom said nervously, looking over at Mathilda.

Mathilda shook her head. "It was my fault," she said. "He might have been dead now because of me."

"No!" Mathew insisted. "You saved his life that time she was taking him away. You stopped her."

"But I didn't know she was the murderer. I thought Maud really loved Danny."

"Why don't we just forget all about it and get ready for lunch," said their mother.

"I just didn't catch on," Mathilda said angrily. "Not even at the end when Mathew fell off the raft, shouting at me to stop, and the cops came. Not even then. I just thought she was the sweetest, kindest old lady I ever met. She was always feeding the ducks, and she always seemed so worried about Danny."

"Because she was afraid he would hurt her precious ducks," Mathew said. "That was it. She only cared for birds. She didn't care at all for people. Not even children. The only reason she killed that crazy man was because he was hurting her ducks, not because he was hurting Danny."

"I know," Uncle Ben said. "I read some of the things she said in the paper. That if humans could behave like birds this would be a much better world. Strange that she would have so much pity for animals and none at all for people."

"She killed them only because she thought they were hurting her birds. Anybody who hurt her birds was her enemy," Mathew said. "The first one was a teenage boy who had run away and, she said, was stealing eggs from the nests. The second one was an old homeless woman who kept taking the bread away from the ducks and geese that Maud fed. She gave them poisoned food. I saw her that time Mathilda and I were sitting up on the top of Strawberry Hill when I was taking off the bands on my teeth."

"Oh, that's right," Mom said. "But Dr. Cummings says he can fit you with new bands next time we see him. Maybe I'll make an appointment for next week."

Mathilda was watching him. He could feel her eyes on him. "No," he said gently to Mom. "I don't want to wear bands."

"But Mathew, your teeth are crooked."

"I know," he said, "but I don't want to wear bands." He smiled almost apologetically at his mother. She was looking at him, bewildered. Ever since they had come home, she'd worn that look of bewilderment on her face. It embarrassed him, and he turned his attention back to his uncle.

"I saw Maud hand the wild man—he was the third

person she killed—something that looked like a piece of cake from up on the hill. They were both standing by themselves on one side of the lake. I saw her do it. I shouldn't have forgotten."

"Well," said their uncle, "you remembered when it was important to remember."

"Yes, he did." Mathilda shook her head. "She was waiting there for us that night when Danny and I jogged over to the boathouse. I should have known because she never came there at night. She was waiting for us. She said she was worried about Danny, and she started asking me lots of questions about where I lived and where my parents were. I didn't catch on. And I didn't tell her anything about me. She must have figured that I was living in the park, and she knew that she couldn't kill Danny unless she killed me too. . . ."

Mathilda stopped talking. Nobody said anything. Not even Dad, who was standing in the doorway now, looking as if he were going to cry.

Mathilda continued. "I told her that the police had taken Rose away. She said yes, she thought that would happen, and that yes, she would take Danny home with her and take good care of him. Danny. Poor kid. He put his arms around her legs, and she patted his head. Then she said in that sweet voice of hers that she'd baked a new angel cake just for the two of us, and she handed each of us a piece. That's when Mathew began shouting and the two cops came flying down the path. One of them even fired a gun, but it was Mathew I heard first. If it weren't for Mathew, Danny and I would have eaten the cake."

"That was the biggest surprise," Mathew said, "that

Joanne and her boyfriend were really cops—under-cover agents. Her boyfriend—I mean, he really wasn't her boyfriend—was pretending to be a jogger that night. He looked familiar, but I didn't recognize him at first. The two of them had become suspicious of Maud, and that night the man had followed her from her house to the park, and Joanne was hiding on one side of the lake. Nobody realized who we were, though. Joanne said she thought Mathilda was kind of a strange boy, but nobody figured out that we were the missing twins. I guess we could have just gone on living there, and nobody would have caught on."

"Or cared." Mathilda had tears in her eyes, and Mom put an arm, very carefully, very uncertainly on her shoulders.

"We cared, darling, Dad and I. But it's all over now, and you're safe at home."

"But lots of people aren't safe," Mathilda said. "It's not right that there are so many people out there who aren't safe, who nobody cares about."

"Mathilda has been keeping in touch with one of the families she met in the park," her father said to Uncle Ben. "That little boy she was so interested in, he'll be coming to pay us a long visit in a week or so."

"Kevin's coming too," Mathilda added, wiping away her tears. "That's his brother. They're both staying with Joanne's mother now, and when Rose and the baby get out of the hospital, I guess they'll stay there too for a while until they find a place for themselves. Joanne's mother is an old lady with a big, empty house, and Joanne says she's been kind of lonely. She does have a cat, but she says she likes people better than animals. The baby was real sick with pneumonia, but she's getting better and better every day."

"We'll have fun with them when they come," Mathew said. "Dad's going to take us all to Marineworld, and I'm going to build a tree house—they'll help me with that. . . ."

"And Dad, you said you'd buy them both Mickey Mouse watches," Mathilda reminded her father. She looked down at the watch on her wrist and said, "I love having my own back again."

"We'll have a good time when they come," Dad promised.

Mathilda said, "I talk to Danny nearly every day. He still doesn't understand about Maud. Maybe it's just as well he doesn't. But I want him to come lots of times. He's like my own family."

"Of course," Mom said quickly. "Of course."

She exchanged a look with Dad who said, "We want to help Danny and his family in every way we can. We want to help them stay together. It was terrible for us when . . . when our family wasn't together. We'll try. I hope we can do it. We'll try."

Mathew looked at his father's face and then looked away quickly. He wondered if things would really change. He wondered what it would be like if his parents no longer shouted at each other, and if he and his father could ever learn to be comfortable with each other. Of one thing he was certain—that whatever else happened between his parents, he and Mathilda would not be separated.

He looked around his empty room and wondered what he could do to fill it. The answer was somewhere buried in his mind, but he knew it was there. It would come to him one day soon. It had better come to him, because if there was one thing he could not stand and never could stand, it was a neat, empty room.

The grown-ups were talking to each other. Mom was saying something unnaturally gentle to his father, and Uncle Ben was murmuring something encouraging to both of them.

Mathilda said to him, "It's so strange living in a house again. We were only in the park one week, and yet I'm still getting used to this house."

This house? Yes, Mathew thought that this house did feel strange. But what kind of house would not feel strange? His head whirled with the thought of all the possible houses one could build in this world—houses made of stone or brick, houses made of skins or reeds, mud houses, thatched houses and tree houses big enough for three or four.

"Everybody should have a house," Mathilda said, "even if it feels strange. Nobody should ever be without a house. When I grow up, I'm going to make sure everybody has a house. Maybe I won't wait until I grow up."

The doorbell rang and their father cried, "Ah— there's our pizza. Let's go, everybody."

Mathilda jumped up and hurried after her father.

"Are you coming, Mathew?" Uncle Ben asked, looking over his shoulder as he passed out of the room.

"Right away," Mathew said. He stood for a moment in the doorway, looking back at the clean, almost empty room and through the window onto the tidy garden. His room was empty, but he felt crowded standing there inside it. Maybe he should go outside after lunch and start working on the tree house he planned to build with Danny and Kevin. His fingers clenched and unclenched as ideas for the tree house and for other houses began crowding into his head.

"Mathew," his mother called, "we're waiting for you."

Yes, he thought to himself as he passed out of the empty room. Yes. I'll go outside and get started on it today.